Tutu Much

Airin Emery

Published by Lechner Syndications

www.lechnersyndications.com

ISBN 13: 978-0-9868825-1-7

"When you dance, your purpose is not to get to a certain place on the floor. It's to enjoy each step along the way."

— Dr. Wayne Dyer

CONTENTS

1   Kelsi   Pg # 1

2   Gisela   Pg # 7

3   Meaghan   Pg # 15

4   Paige   Pg # 23

5   Lori   Pg # 29

6   Meeting in New York   Pg # 35

7   Tap   Pg # 43

8   Roommates   Pg # 49

9   Trouble   Pg # 61

10 Angry Birds   Pg # 67

11   Showcase Auditions   Pg # 71

12 Casting   Pg # 75

13 Body Issues   Pg # 81

14 Pressure   Pg # 87

15 Rehearsal   Pg # 93

16 Rescued by Friendship Pg # 99

17 No Pain, No Gain   Pg # 103

18 The Show Must Go On Pg # 107

19 Showcase   Pg # 111

20 Curtain Call   Pg # 115

AIRIN EMERY

CHAPTER 1: KELSI

"Group four to the floor!" Nick Florez yells. Hundreds of girls fill a large convention center ballroom. Each has a paper number across her stomach.

"That's me," Avelyn says.

Kelsi smiles. Her dimples and perfect teeth stand out against her bright red lipstick. "Good luck!"

"Thanks," Avelyn replies as she makes her way to a square section of wood flooring, taped down near the front, where a group of pre-teen girls and a few guys begin to spread out. Many look nervous and shake out their arms and legs to relax.

"Alright, here we go," Nick says. He nods to an assistant on the side who turns on the sound system. *The Garden* begins to play. The dancers spring to life. Kelsi marks the steps in the back with several other dancers.

Battement, pas de bourré, double. Nick's class is the best. I love lyrical jazz.

Reach, hold. Développé, hold. And contract. I love Co Dance! Competition season rocks.

Kelsi starts to sway her hips a bit, while everyone else concentrates on copying the dancers on the floor. Nick watches the dancers on the floor and makes notes on a pad of paper. A few other faculty members stand on the side and do the same. Judy Rice stands with an older gentleman pointing and gesturing wildly. When he notices Kelsi in the back, he smiles.

The music stops.

"Very good, everyone, very good," Nick says. Everyone claps. Kelsi claps and pushes over her feet to increase the arch.

Alright, I can do this.

The dancers all remain on the wood floor and catch their breath. The people on the side look at the dancers and write quickly in their notepads.

"Next group."

Avelyn strolls toward the back of the room, breathing heavily. Kelsi jogs past her. They wink at one another. Kelsi's long brunette ponytail bounces as she jogs. Glitter falls out with each step. She finds a spot in the center and circles her neck impatiently.

"Alright, here we go!" Nick calls.

Kelsi pulls up the straps of her bedazzled sports bra peeking out above her crop top. The music starts. Kelsi readies herself, right foot crossed back behind the left.

5, 6, 7, 8.

She springs to life, gliding across the room, and hitting every step with power. Kelsi is one of the best dancers on the floor.

Contraction, repeat, repeat.

Kelsi notices Nick isn't paying attention. He talks with another person standing beside him. Determined, she narrows her eyes.

Battement, pas de bourrée, double.

Kelsi gives it everything she's got. Her battement hits the side of her head. She preps for the pirouettes.

Look at me. Look at me!

Kelsi does a perfect triple. Nick sees this and continues to watch her.

She hits her arms out, and then flies through the air with a high Russian, higher than even the guys. She spins around and struts like she's hot stuff.

Take that.

The whole group strikes the final pose. Kelsi purses her lips and looks up. Her false eyelashes and heavy eye shadow make her look like a pop star in concert.

Nick walks into the center and claps.

"Good job dancers," he looks around. "Y'all did a great job. Don't go anywhere, we still have a few minutes. Just give us a second to talk."

Kelsi relaxes and takes a deep breath. Avelyn approaches.

"That was fun, huh?"

Kelsi nods, "Yeah. 'Cept Nick didn't even watch us."

Nick steps away from the group of adults with notepads.

"Alright, I'd like to finish class with the best dancers of the day showing us how it's done. Then, we'll all perform the routine one more time just for fun. Sound good?"

"Yeah!" the group yells.

Nick reads from a piece of paper. "I'd like numbers 17, 22, 48, 89, and 103 to take the floor."

Kelsi turns away and starts to head to the back of the room. Avelyn grabs her.

"Where are you going?"

"It's too crowded up here."

"But you're 103." Avelyn points at Kelsi's number on her stomach.

"What?" Kelsi looks down at the number.

"He called you. Get up there!"

Avelyn pushes Kelsi up to the front. Kelsi looks around, thrilled. She grins widely and takes a place in the back. Nick approaches, grabs her hand and brings her to the front.

"Right here."

Kelsi's eyes widen.

"Think I didn't see that triple?"

He walks away and winks.

"Alright, let's watch these spectacular dancers do their thing!"

All the other students gather around. The music starts. Kelsi moves to the music, ready to begin.

5, 6, 7, 8.

Kelsi shines. She smiles and strikes every movement as if competing. Nick once again isn't paying her enough attention. Kelsi dances even harder. She preps for her pirouette and manages to pull off a quadruple turn, but falls behind a couple beats in the music. Kelsi struggles to catch up and finishes strong.

Everyone claps.

Nick finally turns around and picks up his microphone.

"Everyone one more time."

The music starts right away. All the others are full of energy. Kelsi tries, but she just stares at Nick, Judy and the stranger as she dances. The music stops. Kelsi looks down.

"And, now, the moment you've all been waiting for…" He makes a drum roll sound. All the girls around Kelsi cross their fingers excitedly and bite their lips in anticipation.

"The winner of the scholarship is…number 1…"

Kelsi's eyes light up. "…7." Kelsi looks around, unsure. "Number 17, come on up."

A tiny girl runs up to Nick and hugs him.

"And that's all folks. Thanks for joining us. Hope to see you again next year!"

Several people yell, excitedly. A mob of girls rush up with permanent markers and convention t-shirts in hand. Nick begins signing shirts.

Kelsi walks toward one wall of the room where a bunch of dance bags are scattered. Kelsi grabs her bag and takes off her shoes. She places them in her bag as Avelyn approaches.

"That was so much fun! I can't wait for the next one."

Avelyn grabs her bag.

"Uh huh." Kelsi quickly puts on a pair of Uggs. "You ready?"

"Whoa, what's the rush?"

The elderly man who was talking to Nick approaches behind Kelsi. Avelyn nods to Kelsi signaling her.

"I'm just tired is all."

Avelyn continues to nod her head.

Kelsi looks at her, confused. "Something wrong with your neck?"

"No..." Avelyn nods again.

"Then, why are you doing that?"

The gentleman taps Kelsi's shoulder.

"I believe she was trying to inform you of my presence." His Danish accent is thick and commanding.

Kelsi spins around.

"Oh, yeah, sorry about that."

"No need to apologize. You did nothing wrong."

Kelsi is unsure what to say.

Why is this guy talking to me?

There's an awkward silence.

"I should introduce myself," he says, "I'm Phillipe Morin..."

"The Ballet Master in Chief of the New York Company Ballet," Avelyn cuts in.

Phillipe smiles. "Thank you for the introduction. And you are..."

Kelsi looks at Phillipe in shock. She opens her mouth to speak, but nothing comes out.

Avelyn blurts, "Kelsi."

"I stopped by to visit my friend Judy, and she insisted I see you. We are both very impressed with your technique, Kelsi, and more so your determination on the dance floor."

"Why, thank you," Kelsi manages to stammer out.

"We run a summer program for talented young dancers like you. I'd love it if you'd join us this summer in New York."

Kelsi just stares at him. Avelyn looks at Kelsi's frozen state of shock and shakes her arm.

"Kels," she shakes her again, "he just asked you to go to New York."

Kelsi snaps out of her state of shock.

"Wow...I mean I don't know what to say. I mean, yes."

She jumps up excitedly. "Yes, I'd love to go!"

Kelsi hugs Avelyn, then turns and composes herself in a second. She faces Phillipe.

"Thank you very much for this opportunity. I am truly honored."

He smiles. "You've earned it. I think you'll find the school very beneficial in the development of your skills and ballet education."

Kelsi nods her head, "Yes, my ballet education."

Ballet education.

"Yes, you **do** realize the curriculum is entirely ballet focused."

All ballet.

"A background rich in ballet will enable you to grow far more quickly than any traditional genre training. You can do anything in the dance world with proper ballet technique."

"Yes, sir," Kelsi agrees.

Phillippe hands her a business card.

"Call this number and give them your information. We'll be in contact with you after that."

Kelsi takes the card and smiles.

"Very nice to meet you, Kelsi." He extends his hand. Kelsi shakes it.

"Same to you. And thank you. Thank you, so much."

"You're very welcome."

Phillipe walks off. Kelsi turns to Avelyn whose jaw drops and lets out a silent scream.

"Oh, my god!"

"I know, right?" Kelsi says.

"You're so lucky. You're not only going to a real ballet school. You're going to 'the' ballet school." Avelyn squeals. "Wait 'til Sabine hears about this. She's gonna be so jealous. You can rub this all in her face. Take that Miss Diva."

A professional ballet school. Yikes!

Kelsi smiles at Avelyn and nods as Avelyn continues to talk.

Professional ballerinas?

"Congratulations, bestie!"

Avelyn tightly squeezes Kelsi.

"Thanks."

New York Company Ballet, here I come!

CHAPTER 2: GISELA

"Wait up, Gisela!" Tatiana calls. Toting a large purse, she dashes out the subway doors into the station.

"It's Zel, mother." Gisela rolls her dark brown eyes. "For the millionth time," she mumbles under her breath.

"Your birth certificate said Gisela for a reason. Named after the classic Giselle, it's your destiny," Tatiana recants.

Gisela walks swiftly through the tunnel and up a flight up stairs, to the streets of New York City.

"This is the first year you're able to attend the intensive, I want you to take this seriously. Did you know a million girls across the world wished they danced at the New York Company Ballet? You get to dance there every day."

"Did you know tap dancers have on average a 15 year longer career than ballerinas?" Gisela snaps back.

"Ballet is in your blood…"

"Says the former prima ballerina."

Tatiana stops at the base of a set of stairs, leading to a large building. Gisela heads up the stairs.

"Zel!" Tatiana calls.

Gisela stops and turns around.

"You can do this," Tatiana's eyes plead.

Gisela nods and continues to head up the stairs.

Let's just hope this goes quickly.

* * * * * * * * * * * * * * * * * *

A large ballet studio is filled with numerous young ballet dancers at the barre. Each has a number across her black leotard.

Gisela performs a simple warm-up sequence of plies and coordinating arms at the barre. Her turnout and posture are effortlessly perfect. She glances at the clock. It reads 2:45.

One hour to get out of here.

* * * * * * * * * * * * * * * * * * * *

"Those of you remaining are our finalists. We'd like to see a short combination, and following that, we'll be able to decide if we'd like to invite anyone to join us this summer," a thin, petite woman says.

A waif-like ballet dancer steps in front of the girls and demonstrates a combination. Gisela watches, with half-interest, from the back. She glances at the clock once more. It reads 3:30.

The petite woman watches the girls mark their steps as the waif performs the combination once more. Gisela doesn't even mark a step. She tilts her head side- to- side and watches the dancer's feet, then yawns.

"Alright, that's it. No questions. No rehearsal. Let's see who can learn at this speed because, well ladies, you got lucky. Normally I don't even repeat it."

The girls scurry to the corner. The thin woman nods to a pianist in the corner and the first group takes off across the floor. The girls struggle with the sequence and it's obvious they're thinking deeply about what comes next.

Gisela steps up to the center of the next group. She takes off, fiery. She hits every plie and tendu perfectly. She is, however emotionless and obviously uninterested with the combination.

Gisela finishes and walks past the thin woman. The woman watches her walk to the other side of the room. The angular ballerina beside her leans in, "spitting image of her mother's style."

The thin woman nods.

"Just a darker version."

Gisela paces in a corner as she looks at the clock.

* * * * * * * * * * * * * * * * * * * *

"Thank you all for coming," the thin woman says.

Only fifteen ballet dancers still remain. They are all lined up against one barre.

"This final group was by far the best of the day," she continues.

Gisela leans against the barre and casually moves her feet, doing tap rifts and not paying attention to what is being said.

8

"As you're all aware, our school is extremely prestigious so we have to be very selective in the type of dancer we admit to the summer program. This year, while you are all fine dancers, only one person in this session meets our strict requirements."

The other dancers all look around at one another. Several cross their fingers and wait with bated breath.

"Congratulations, Gisela Palente."

The others all sigh, and suddenly sulk a bit, but try to act happy and clap for her. Gisela hardly looks up. The dancer beside her pats Gisela's back.

"Good job. You're so lucky!"

Gisela looks around and realizes what's going on. She smiles at the thin woman.

"Thank you all for coming. We hope to see you again next year."

The dancers crowd Gisela and congratulate her.

"You're so amazing. You deserve it."

"You're so fortunate. I'm jealous."

"Congrats!"

"Where do you dance?"

Gisela pushes through the group to grab her dance bag in the corner of the room. She grabs it and starts to leave. The thin woman cuts her off.

"We're honored to have the daughter of such an extraordinary performer in our intensive. I hope that you're ready for a lot of hard work."

Gisela nervously shifts, "Yeah…course…of course I am."

She looks at the clock. It reads 3:45.

"Is your mother here? I'd love to talk with her about some things for the summer performance."

"Probably. She's likely in the hall listening right now."

Gisela looks at the clock again.

"I really have to go. Thank you very much for this opportunity."

She rushes out the door. Tatiana is right next to the door. She throws her arms around Gisela.

"I'm so proud of you, Gisela!"

"Zel."

"I knew you could do it."

Gisela tries to move out of her reach.

"Let's celebrate! Non-fat frozen yogurts?"

"I have to go."

"But honey, we have so much to talk about. You'll need to take at least another two classes a week to get ready."

Gisela's jaw drops. "I already take 7 ballet classes a week."

"Perfection is learned."

Gisela rolls her eyes, "I have tap. Talk to Madame Violet. She's dying to speak with you."

Gisela takes off down the stairs, "Bye."

Tatiana watches her jog down, then enters the dance room.

* * * * * * * * * * * * * * * * * * * *

Gisela's pink tights poke out from under her black warm-up pants. She leans forward from her subway seat and tugs at the end of her pants to cover the tights. A man sitting across from her looks at her oddly. She smirks and then casually removes a hair tie to release her tight bun. Her long, dark locks fall and she looks like a young Selma Hayek. The man across from her suddenly smiles. She frowns and looks at her cell phone. The time on it reads 3:58.

The subway comes to a stop. The rolling screen at the top of the doors says "Broadway." Gisela hops up, with her bag in hand, and runs through the doors as they open.

* * * * * * * * * * * * * * * * * * * *

"A five, six, seven, eight." Alan claps out the beats of an upbeat jazzy song.

Several guys and girls of varying ages tap in a small dimly-lit studio.

Alan, an older lanky man, lively taps his toe, moves with the music, and claps to the rhythm.

Gisela sneaks in through the back door, trying not to be seen. She tip-toes in her tap shoes and joins in behind a couple of happy tappers.

Ah, the combination from last week. I remember that one.

Alan spots her as he claps. Gisela doesn't make eye contact as she jumps right into the dance. A huge grin comes across her face as her whole body relaxes, and she just lets go of all her worries.

And a one, two, three, flap, heel dig. Time step and down. And down. And down.

All the dancers finish with a set of wings. Gisela's arms circle quickly and she completes 8 wings with ease. The music stops.

Everyone smiles or giggles. Gisela lets out a deep breath and smiles.

"Very good. Glad to see you have your thinking caps on today," Alan laughs. "Try this one on for size."

Alan begins a complicated sequence of rifts and shuffles. All the dancers' eyes are glued on his feet. Alan drags his right toe into his ankle and spins.

"Any questions?"

Everyone shakes their head "no."

Gisela raises her hand.

"Yes, Zel."

"Regular or double time?" She inquires.

A couple of the other dancers giggle.

"I'm not sure you can do it double-time. Why don't we try it at regular tempo first?"

Gisela frowns.

"Any other questions?" Alan asks. "If not let's…"

Gisela breaks into the sequence by herself, double-time. Alan stops mid sentence. He watches her feet move at lightning speed. She is calm and collected as she hits each rift. The other dancers watch with amazement. Alan steps closer and moves through the small cluster of spectator tappers. Gisela finishes, strikes her heel against the floor, and excitedly throws her arms outward.

"Ah ha!" She exclaims.

I did it. I knew I could!

The room falls silent. The others look at Alan awaiting a reaction. His face is expressionless.

Well…

Finally, he purses his lips, "That last step was wrong."

Gisela's face drops.

What?

Alan turns and walks back to the front of the room.

That's it? But I just did it. I did it double-time.

Her forehead wrinkles as she stares at him, confused.

"Let's start again, regular tempo, please."

The music starts. Everyone dances; Gisela moves with the music but she continues to stare at Alan.

I don't get it.

He looks at her and winks. His lips crack a smile.

Oh darn you, Alan. I knew it!

She continues to dance, relaxed and carefree.

Alan smiles. Gisela smiles back.

God, I love tap!

* * * * * * * * * * * * * * * * *

The dancers all gather their things and talk. A teen boy, Derek, sits on the floor beside Gisela and takes off his shoes.

"That was pretty brave what you did?"

Gisela smiles, "Nah. Anyone would do it."

"I never would've just done it like that. I can hardly get it regular tempo, much less double-time. You were pretty awesome."

"Thanks." She reaches out her hand. "I'm Zel."

"Derek."

"Derek, nice to meet you."

"You've been dancing here long?" he asks.

Gisela shakes her head, "Two years."

"Where did you tap before that?"

"I didn't."

Derek is shocked. He starts to open his mouth to respond, but Alan walks over.

"I'd like to remind everyone we're hosting an intensive for the very first time this summer, and I'd love for all of you to attend the auditions. Even if you don't plan on doing the summer program, it's a great experience to start practicing the audition process so you don't 'choke'. He pretends to pull a noose around his neck and sticks out his tongue, and continues talking. "You know when the real thing comes around."

Gisela stares at him, her eyes full of excitement and at the same time, sadness.

She'll never let me go.

"Auditions start at 9 am, three weeks from Saturday."

Three weeks. Maybe I can make this work.

"Nice to meet you, Zel. I gotta run, Mom's outside waiting," Derek says.

Gisela is in a daze. He waves goodbye and she pops out of her daze.

"Oh yeah, hi, I mean bye."

Gisela grabs her bag and stands up to leave. Alan stops her.

"I trust you'll be at the auditions."

Gisela bites her lip.

"You see, I'd like to but..."

"No buts," he interrupts.

"But my..."

Alan puts up his finger and cuts her off.

"Not just anyone can do double-time after visually memorizing a combination. That's not skill, that's a God-given talent."

Gisela sighs.

"Thank you for the class. I really enjoyed myself."

"Put it on your calendar," Alan responds.

Gisela turns away.

I have to go. I know I'll get in. If I get in here, then I won't have to do the ballet one.

Gisela smiles, dreamily as she walks out of the room.

A whole summer of tap.

Her smile widens. She jumps with excitement.

I'm doin' this!

Gisela walks down a street and heads back to the subway.

Time to start plotting.

CHAPTER 3: MEAGHAN

"Wipe on. Wipe off. Wipe on. Wipe off." Meaghan's plump fingers clean the mirrored wall of a dance studio. She stares at herself in the mirror for a moment. Her frizzy, red hair is disheveled and her green eyes stand out against her freckled cheeks.

"Introducing, Meaghan Gerardi. World famous ballerina," she boasts in a deep tone.

Meaghan clutches a bottle of Windex and roll of paper towels against her chest as she turns emotional.

"Thank you, thank you, you're far too kind."

She stands tall and proud and returns to the deep masculine tone, "And now Meaghan will premiere an original piece, sure to be applauded worldwide."

Meaghan nods bashfully then takes a couple steps back and begins to dance gracefully.

Hmmm.Hmmmm.Laa dumdee daaa…

Balance, balance, glissade, sous sous.

Hmmmmm hmmmmm la lal la la lala laaaaaa…

Meaghan continues to dance around, humming and singing and lost in the utter joy of just dancing. She continues to hold the Windex bottle and paper towels. Miss Jenny, a petite woman in her early forties, stands in the doorway and watches.

"So, this is what you really do on Sundays."

Meaghan freezes. She blushes instantly with her red cheeks match her hair.

"I…I was just…," she starts.

"Reminds me of when you first came here. Dancing around with your Angelina Ballerina doll." Miss Jenny smiles. "I bet you still have that doll."

Meaghan nods.

"I was just going to finish the mirrors. I'm sorry. I got carried away."

"What song was it today?"

"*Cheek to Cheek.*"

"Ah, a classic. Long before your time. Your mom plays that one I assume?"

Meaghan nods again. "She loves Frank Sinatra."

"Who doesn't?" Miss Jenny replies.

Meaghan looks down at the cleaning supplies in-hand, and then at Miss Jenny.

"I'll go ahead and finish those mirrors now."

She darts toward the mirror.

"You can practice. Practice makes perfect, you know."

"Yes, ma'am."

"And I know there's a very special day coming up soon."

Meaghan raises an eyebrow.

"The New York Company Ballet? You still plan on going, right?"

Meaghan sighs.

"Denver's a long way away from Boulder City, just for an audition, and I can't afford to get there. Plus, even if I did get in to the school, it's in New York, and there's no way we could pay for it. That's more than my mom makes in a month. So, it's kinda silly to go. Just another dream," she sadly says, shrugging her shoulders and looking down.

"Not necessarily."

Meaghan looks up.

"I submitted that tape you made a couple months ago to a few scholarship contests."

Meaghan's eyes brighten.

"Turns out someone liked what they saw. You won a scholarship." Miss Jenny pulls out an envelope tucked in the back of her pants. She hands it to Meaghan and smiles, "Congratulations!"

Meaghan jumps into the air, grabs Miss Jenny, and wraps her arms around her.

"Thank you, thank you so much!" Meaghan jumps again. "Wait! Is this real? Are you kidding? I won a ballet scholarship? Well, I mean money to travel to audition for a ballet scholarship?!"

"See for yourself," Miss Jenny points to the envelope.

Meaghan nervously looks at the envelope.

"But I don't deserve this. There are so many other girls..."

"There are lots of other girls. This is yours. Enjoy it," Miss Jenny reassures. "Besides, it's not all that much, but certainly enough to get you there and back."

Meaghan takes a deep breath. She opens the envelope and pulls out a folded piece of paper. She unfolds the paper and inside is a check and note. The check is written out for five hundred dollars. The letter is on Colorado Chamber of Commerce letterhead. Meaghan looks up at Miss Jenny and grins.

"Just a random scholarship, huh?" she asks.

"The chamber needed to award some money. You were the best candidate," Miss Jenny replies.

"And your husband being the President of the Chamber has nothing to do with it?"

Miss Jenny shrugs, "Nothing at all." She breaks a smile. "Just enjoy it. You need to do this."

"Thanks. I'll practice really hard."

"I know you will. The whole town's counting on you."

Meaghan looks down at the check again.

The whole town? I can't let them down. I'm gonna make my mom proud.

"Thanks, Miss Jenny. This means a whole lot to me."

"I know," she says. "Now get on with that practicing."

Meaghan smiles and sets down the bottle of Windex and paper towel roll.

"After you finish the mirrors, of course," Miss Jenny adds.

Meaghan blushes again and picks up the cleaning supplies. She walks over to a mirror and sprays it. Miss Jenny starts to leave the room.

She stops in the doorway and turns back, "Watch your turnout in your left inside pirouettes."

Meaghan nods, "Okay."

"Oh, and keep working those feet."

"Right."

Miss Jenny leaves the room.

Meaghan looks down at her flat, barefoot feet.

Come on feet. Help me out here.

* * * * * * * * * * * * * * * * * *

Meaghan tightens a rope around the insole of her right foot. The other end of the rope is tied to the post at the end of her bed. Her left foot is already tied. She leans back. Her toes arch over.

"A little more."

She sits up and tightens the knot even more.

Do it. Do it.

She leans back. Her toes arch even further this time.

Agghh. That hurts...just a little.
She closes her eyes.
New York City. New York City.
She opens her eyes.
"I can do this. Just think good thoughts. Time to fall fast asleep."
She closes her eyes again.

* * * * * * * * * * * * * * * *

"Plie and straighten. Plie and straighten. Grande plie and up,"
a blonde woman with a thick Russian accent calls out.
Meaghan goes into her grande plie. The Russian woman taps her bottom with a ruler. "Tuck under."
Meaghan holds her breath and squeezes her butt further under hips.
Squeeze!
"Turn out from the hips." The woman presses against Meaghan's hips and forces them outward.
Meaghan grits her teeth and continues to hold her breath.
Open hips!
The paper number fastened to her leotard crumples loudly. She opens her arms out to second position.
"Elbows up." She taps Meaghan's slightly sagging elbow.
Breathe, breathe.
Stiff as a board, Meaghan continues the combination. She keeps her eyes forward as they well with tears.
Boulder City is counting on me. Step up your game, Meg.

* * * * * * * * * * * * * * * * *

Out on the center of the room, the dancers perform an entrechat and changement combination. Meaghan stands out with her red hair and freckles.
"Close your fifths number twenty-two!" the Russian woman yells.
Meaghan looks in the mirror at the number 22 across her abdomen. She takes another deep breath and tries to tighten her closures upon landing. The music stops.
"That's all for today, ladies."
The dancers all politely clap.
That was a disaster.
"You'll be notified by mail if you've been accepted."
She curtsies and the others follow. Meaghan curtsies as well and then

walks toward the door with her head down.

I was terrible. What was I thinking? I shouldn't have come in the first place.

She sniffs. Her eyes are glossy with tears. The other girls move slowly through the door. Meaghan shifts her feet, anxious to get out.

What will I tell Miss Jenny?

She looks around, scared.

I'm such a loser. Bad feet. Bad posture. No turnout. Bad arms.

She looks sideways in the mirror. All the girls around her are rail thin and barely visible in the mirror when standing in profile. Her body is clearly visible. Her curvy waist, arched back and blossoming chest stand out.

And I'm fat.

She slumps and sighs.

As she exits the room, a few girls behind her chat.

"How was it for you?"

The girl rolls her eyes. "I hope ABT is better or I might not be doing a summer intensive this year."

"I know she didn't even hardly look at me."

"Me neither. And I have my best Grishkos on today. Everyone loves these shoes. My arch looks incredible in these."

"I wish I had gotten noticed like that redhead."

Meaghan's ears perk up.

Redhead?

She looks around, there's no one else with red hair.

"I know, huh?"

Does she mean me?

"They were all over her. She practically had a private."

"I know, I'm so jealous."

Jealous? Why would they be jealous? The teacher hated me. I did everything wrong.

Meaghan slows her pace in leaving the building. She stops outside the building and looks back.

Huh? Maybe that was okay.

She puts her hand up in the air to hail a cab.

Did they actually like me?

A taxi stops for her. She opens the door.

Was that a good thing?

"Where you headed?" the taxi driver asks.

Did they like me?

"Destination?" the driver questions again.

Meaghan shakes her head. "Oh, Denver Airport please."

Maybe any attention is good.

Her frown turns upside down and she starts to smile.

It has to be. I did well.
Meaghan beams with pride. Her cheeks glow radiantly.
I'm so proud of myself.
"Yeah!"
The taxi driver looks in his rear view mirror at Meaghan pumping her fist in the air. He raises an eyebrow and shakes his head.

* * * * * * * * * * * * * * * * * * *

"Mail, honey!" Meaghan's mom calls down the hallway.
Meaghan pokes her head through a door. "I'll be there later. I'm getting ready for class."
"There's something here you might like." She waves an envelope in the air.
Meaghan freezes. Her mom smiles. Meaghan darts down the hall.
"Whoa hold your horses there, young lady."
Meaghan grabs the envelope out of her hand. The sender's name reads "New York Company Ballet – Summer Intensive."
Meaghan stares at the envelope. Her mother watches with baited breath.
"Open it already."
Meaghan turns to her mom. "Mom, would you mind if I wait and open it with Miss Jenny?"
Meaghan's mother's smile fades. She nods her head slowly, "Sure sweetheart. If that's what you want to do."
Meaghan nods, "It's just that she made this happen, you know with the scholarship and all."
Her mom wraps her arms around her. "I'm really proud of you."
"Thanks, mom."
"For everything. You've worked so hard to make my dreams come true."
She stares into her daughter's eyes, her own well with tears.
"Your father wanted nothing more than to see you in these moments. He would have been so proud."
"I know."
Meaghan hugs her mom, "I love you, mom."
"Love you too, sweetheart."

* * * * * * * * * * * * * * * * * * *

Miss Jenny and Meaghan stand in the dance studio together. A couple girls stretch at the barre and on the floor before class. Meaghan hands Miss Jenny the envelope.

"I want you to do it."

Miss Jenny raises an eyebrow. "You sure?"

Meaghan nods. "Positive."

"Okay, here we go."

Miss Jenny carefully opens the envelope.

"Read it out loud."

Miss Jenny unfolds the paper and begins to read: "Dear Meaghan Gerardi, we were very impressed with your performance during our auditions, however, due to limited space we are unable to invite you at this time."

Meaghan's face is blank.

"You have been placed on a waitlist."

Miss Jenny looks up from the paper. The other girls look over at them.

"You did great. You should be proud of yourself."

Meaghan can't even look her in the eyes.

No.

"You can try again next year. You'll be in for sure."

No. I can't believe I did this.

Miss Jenny pats her back.

I let everyone down.

"I let everyone down."

Miss Jenny looks at her and shakes her head. "Why would you say that?"

"I'm so sorry."

"Oh honey, you tried your best, that's all anyone can ask."

Meaghan continues to shake her head.

No.

"I'm sorry. I don't think I can make it to class today."

Meaghan runs out of the room. Miss Jenny calls after her. "Meaghan!" She continues to run.

CHAPTER 4: PAIGE

Classical music plays. A large bedroom suite is in impeccable condition. The walls are white but decorated with original paintings of ballerinas. In the center of one wall is an original Degas housed in a gold frame. Wood flooring covers one side of the room. A barre is affixed to a mirrored wall. Paige Ling, a beautiful slim mixed Japanese -Caucasian girl of fourteen years stands with one hand on the barre and the other in high fifth. Her right leg extends in second, mere inches from her head. She taps the barre lightly with her left hand to check her balance.

Weight over the toes.

Paige releases her left hand and gracefully lifts it to high fifth. Her long neck stretches upward and her defined collarbone pops out. She holds the pose for several seconds. Her feet arch over perfectly.

There's a knock at the door.

So much for concentration.

"Come in," she says.

An older Japanese woman opens the door.

"Paisley is here for your massage, and Tania would like to know if you're ready for a training session immediately following?"

Paige lowers her leg to the ground slowly with the utmost control.

"Send Paisley in. And let Tania know I can only do half an hour today. I have an audition to prepare for."

The woman bows and closes the door.

Paige examines her body in the mirror. She places her hands around her waist and pushes her six-pack abs in. She sucks in further. Her waist completely disappears.

Paisley enters the room with a massage table.

"Good morning, Paige."

"Morning."

"What needs work today?"

Paisley sets up the table in the middle of the room.

"Let's just relax my calves; they're a bit stiff today. I'm having trouble fully extending."

"Calves, it is."

Paige lies face down on the massage table, her face pokes through the cut-out hole of the table.. Paisley rubs oil on her hands and begins to massage the backs of her calves.

"So, big audition today?"

One of many.

"Yes. It is the New York Company Ballet one today."

"You all ready?"

No, there's something I need to do first.

* * * * * * * * * * * * * * * * * *

A toilet flushes. Paige walks out of the toilet section of bathroom and over to a scale beside the sink. She steps up on it and releases a deep breath of air. She looks down at the scale; it reads 88.

88? I was 87 yesterday.

Paige steps down from the scale. She takes in a deep breath of air and then releases it completely. She steps back on the scale. It reads 88.

This is not happening.

She looks in the mirror and notices a little bit of cleavage showing out of her leotard. She shakes her head and opens a medicine cabinet.

Her long, thin fingers search for the right thing. They stop over a roll of medical gauze.

I can take care of this little problem.

Paige wraps medical gauze around her ribs, flattening her chest. She pulls her leotard back up to cover the wrapping and looks in the mirror. Her frame is now flat from top to bottom.

There. Perfect.

* * * * * * * * * * * * * * * * * *

"Bowl on the counter is for you, Miss Paige," the older Japanese woman says.

"Thank you, Nini."

Paige walks over to the enormous granite counter and sits on a modern-

24

looking bar stool.

Great. Potstickers. Full of fat.

Nini places a hand on Paige's shoulder, "Your favorite." She smiles widely. Paige smiles politely.

"I think I'll save these for later," Paige says. "I just want a little snack for now."

Paige wanders into the kitchen and opens a large custom built-in fridge door. She pulls out a handful of grapes and sets them on a plate. Standing at the counter, she pushes one grape at a time to one side of the plate.

Five grapes are 30 calories. I can afford to have 80 calories right now.

She pushes a few more grapes to the side.

Actually, I should only do 60.

She pushes a couple grapes back the other way. Ten grapes are on one side of the plate. She places one in her mouth and chews very slowly.

"Miss Paige, you should eat more than that. You have a lot of dancing to do."

Paige continues to chew her first grape, she shakes her head, "Nah, this is just right. Trust me."

55 to go.

She places another grape in her mouth.

* * * * * * * * * * * * * * * * * * *

A limousine exits a gated property and pulls out onto a highway. A sign along the side of the road reads: YOU ARE NOW LEAVING MALIBU.

Inside the limousine, Paige looks into a drop down mirror as Nini slicks back her hair and twists it into a bun.

"What's our time looking like, Miguel?" Paige asks the man driving up front.

"Plenty of time, Miss Paige. You'll arrive with lots of time to stretch."

"Thank you, Miguel."

She looks in the mirror.

"Can you make it tighter on the left side, it feels a tad loose."

Nini rebrushes one side of Paige's head and tightens the hair tie.

* * * * * * * * * * * * * * * * * *

Paige dances across the floor like a graceful swan. Despite her tiny size, she looks much older due to her ease of movement and almond-shaped LucyLui eyes which gently guide her focus.

Tombé pas de bourrée, relève, double reverse attitude.

She closes to fifth position.

Phillipe Morin leans into the small Russian woman and whispers, "Number 60. Immediate action."

He walks out of the room. The Russian woman steps forward. "Thank you all. Letters will be sent out in the mail over the next few weeks. Number 60, would you mind staying for a moment, please?"

The dancers all curtsy and clap, then gather their things and leave.

Paige tiptoes over to the Russian woman, "Yes, ma'am, you asked me to stay?"

The Russian woman grins.

"Yes, precious child. Turn a second for me."

Paige slowly turns around.

"Perfect body, perfect feet. You are a dream."

Paige is emotionless.

"We'd like to give you automatic entrance to the school. Normally we send out letters, but Mr. Morin himself requested we tell you immediately. Welcome to the NYCB intensive."

"Thank you," Paige says, quitereserved.

"You have impressed us all."

Paige curtsies.

"Your parents must be very proud."

Paige frowns.

Yeah.

"I'm very excited to be asked, thank you very much."

Paige turns and walks out of the room.

* * * * * * * * * * * * * * * *

Paige sits in the back of the limousine all by herself.

Mother said she would be here. I have no one to share my excitement with. No one who really knows me. No one who really cares.

"So, how did it go?" Miguel asks as he drives.

"Great. I got in."

"That's good news."

He's paid to care.

"You should be smiling," he smiles in the rear view mirror back at her.

Paige flashes him a fake smile.

"I'm a bit tired, I'm gonna take a nap now."

She pushes a button and the partition between Miguel and the back of the limo closes.

Paige sinks into the seat, puts her iPod ear buds in and closes her eyes.

I need something good right now. Something to make me feel full.

* * * * * * * * * * * * * * * * *

Paige sits on a large, plush bed with a spoon dug into a quart of ice cream. She scrapes the bottom of the container and eats every last drop.

Ah, now that's good.

A full bag of chips lies at her feet. Paige sets the empty ice cream container on the nightstand and grabs the bag of chips.

"Sweet down, onto salty."

She tears open the bag of chips and smells the contents. She takes one out and places it on her tongue.

Ah, delicious.

Paige begins to shovel the chips into her mouth. She lies back and continues to eat.

* * * * * * * * * * * * * * * * *

Paige stands in the bathroom and brushes her long hair. She pulls it back into a ponytail and then enters the toilet section.

She begins to vomit. The sound is disgusting and she continues over and over again. Finally, she emerges from the restroom and looks back in the mirror at herself.

Might need another round.

Paige steps up on the scale. It reads 87.

Three more pounds to go for summer.

She steps down and walks back into the toilet section. The vomiting continues.

CHAPTER 5: LORI

"Aren't you gonna open them?" Jody asks. Lori raises her eyes from the perfectly-made bunk bed with four evenly spaced envelopes sitting on it. She inserts a bobby pin in her bun, then shakes her head. Her slicked- back blonde hair doesn't even move.

"Why not?" Jody pries.

Lori shrugs, "I don't know. I'm staying here, so there's not really a point." She stretches out her slender legs and spots the end of a pink ribbon, poking out of the tied knot above her ankle.

"Stickies." Jody hands her a sheet of small clear square stickers. Lori peels one off and attaches it to the back of the flapping ribbon. She carefully tucks the ribbon end under the knot. "There."

"It's just class you know," Jody smirks. She adjusts her own ribbons. A piece of mole skin covers the toe of the pointe shoe.

"You put mole skin on again? It's no wonder you're having trouble on your pirouettes."

"It helps. Honestly." Jodie pulls leg warmers over her shoes and stands up. "Not all of us are born to turn like you."

"Not born, just on balance," Lori replies.

"Yeah, whatever."

Lori smiles knowingly. "Your spotting's getting better. I saw that snap in class this morning."

Jody laughs, "Yeah right before I hit poor Andre in the face. My high fifth arms just weren't happening." They both chuckle. "Guess that's what summer camp is for, right?"

Lori's smile fades; she looks at the envelopes on the bed. Jody looks at the clock; it reads "3:48."

"Yikes, we're gonna be late. Got your flats?"

Lori faintly nods and holds up a pair of ballet slippers. Jody opens the door and begins to walk out. Lori looks back at the envelopes. She bites her lip and starts to reach for one. She stops and quickly heads out the door behind Jody.

* * * * * * * * * * * * * * * * * *

"Entrechat, entrechat, entrechat, jeté. Tombé pas de bourrée, pas de chat, sous sous, glissade, glissade, grand jeté, arms seconde. Then piqué to third arabesque and hold." Anita Young, the senior ballet instructor nods to Lori.

Lori closes her fifth position tightly, presents her arms out then lowers to first and lifts her torso. The piano player in the corner, Andre, begins to play. Lori comes to life with the music. Her chin perks up and she performs the combination flawlessly. All the other students watch, a couple mark the sequence on the side as she dances.

Lori piqués to arabesque in her ballet slippers and holds it for several seconds. Her balance is impeccable and she holds the position effortlessly. She smiles proudly, full of grace. Anita raises her hand to Andre and the music stops. Lori releases out of the arabesque and finishes. The other students clap politely.

"Thank you, Lori." Lori nods, bashfully.

"Any questions?" The other students all shake their heads. "Alright then, three at a time from the corner."

The students scurry to the corner. Lori starts to follow while Anita walks beside her for a step. "Sorry you won't be joining us this summer." Anita walks toward the mirror to watch.

Lori freezes, her face drops as she loses all composure. She opens her mouth to respond but the music begins and the first set of girls begin across the floor dancing the combination.

Why would she say that? Not staying here for the summer intensive? But…oh wait…

Lori watches the other girls and scowls. Her forehead wrinkles up and she grimaces. Jody moves over beside her in line and elbows her. "What gives?"

"Huh?"

"What's up with the wrinkle face?"

Lori looks at her, unsure. Jody mocks her and scrunches her face up tight. Monique, another girl, chuckles. Anita looks over at the girls and raises an eyebrow. The girls all straighten up and stare straight ahead.

Jody whispers, "What is it?" Lori is in a daze.

…how would she know? I haven't made a decision yet. I love England.

Jody elbows her again. "I love England." Lori stammers.

Jody's eyes widen, she covers her mouth to hold back a laugh. "Me too…you're up."

Lori looks around, lost. She steps forward and takes her place with two other girls. They all close to a tight fifth position, present their arms, then take off across the floor performing the combination. Lori dances perfectly, but her face is blank. She stares at Anita as she dances.

Maybe they're not taking me back…but I'm the best dancer here this year. Maybe…

She piqués to her arabesque and holds it. The other girls step down and move aside. Lori continues to hold her arabesque as she thinks.

Oh no, they wouldn't.

The next set of girls, including Jody and Monique, dance across the floor. Jody looks to the side and sees Lori still holding her arabesque. The other two girls don't see her as they stare ahead at the mirrors.

They couldn't.

Monique spots Jody as she prepares for her grand jeté. "Psst." Lori doesn't budge.

Monique moves slightly forward on her grand jeté and Jody moves back, but the third girl, Rebecca doesn't see Lori at all.

All of a sudden, Lori's face lights up, her eyes widen. *My parents!* Just then Rebecca jetés right into her. Crash! They both fall down.

"Show off!" Rebecca stammers.

"What? Huh?" Lori shakes her head, unsure what just happened. The music stops. Anita walks over.

Rebecca grabs her ankle in pain. "Look at what you did! Now my summer solo chances are ruined."

Anita squats down and touches the ankle.

"Do you need a medic?"

Rebecca nods. Anita sighs.

"Alright. Monique, will you take Rebecca to the medic, please?"

"Sure."

Monique helps Rebecca up and slings Rebecca's arm over her shoulder. Anita looks at Lori sternly. Lori lowers her eyes.

* * * * * * * * * * * * * * * * *

"How could you do that?!" Lori yells at her laptop computer. On the screen are her mother and father, Mr. and Mrs. Clark.

"Calm down, darling," Mr. Clark says. He sits with his wife on a designer sofa in an upscale home. The Clarks lived in upstate New York and had done well in the real estate market when Lori was just a baby. Basically, they were filthy rich. Lori had always had a nanny and was shipped off to boarding school at the Royal Academy when she was eight years old so ballet was all she knew.

"Calm down? I told you I wanted to stay in England. The Royal Academy is the best in the world." Lori waves her arms around showcasing all the Royal Academy Ballet posters on the walls.

"I think you're exaggerating a bit, Lori," Mrs. Clark rolls her eyes. "Ask your sisters; the National Ballet of Canada and Miami Ballet are far better."

"You just say that because they're company members there."

"No, Nadine was just promoted to soloist."

Lori picks up a Royal Academy of Ballet folder with photos of her, Jody and Monique plastered on the front. She holds it in front of the screen for them to see.

"But, my friends are here."

"You have other friends," her father recants.

"Not ballet friends."

"Enough of the temper tantrums young lady, we've dealt with more than our fair share of that."

"Really, mom? You've made every decision in my life. I never got to choose," Lori crosses her arms, defiantly.

Mrs. Clark replies,, "Fine you can have a choice now."

Lori's face brightens. She sits up straight.

"Really?"

"You're coming home, so pick a camp," her mother finishes.

"That's it. So I get no say?"

"I just gave you a choice."

"What kind of choice is it,if you already took away what I want?"

Lori rolls her eyes and starts to pace the room.

"You heard your mother, back to the States, young lady."

"Well, I have to go. Darcie and I have appointments at the spa. Ta ta, sweetheart."

Lori half-waves, but doesn't even turn to look at the screen. Mrs. Clark walks away. Mr. Clark moves closer to the screen.

"Listen honey, just come home this summer and maybe next summer you can pick another school or stay there. Alright?"

Lori nods, tears well in her eyes.

"Miss you."

Lori sniffles and fights back a tear.

"Miss you too, daddy."

Mr. Clark wiggles his nose. Lori smiles. She wiggles her nose back. *Eskimo kisses.*

Lori sighs and sits on the bed.

Mr. Clark waves good-bye. The screen goes dark. Lori closes the laptop.

She falls back on her bed and lets out a sigh.

Peace and quiet.

The door swings open. Monique skips in, followed by Jody.

Monique hops on Lori's bed.

"Hey there, Twinkle Toes!"

Lori sits up.

"Ha, ha, very funny."

Jody sits on the bed across from them and takes off her shoes. All three girls suddenly scowl. Lori and Monique grab pillows to cover their faces.

"Agghhh, make it stop." Monique squirms. She fans the pillow in front of her face. Jody holds her nose and moves her shoes over toward the door.

"Sanitize!" Lori calls.

Jody grabs a bottle of body spray and squirts the shoes.

"More!" Monique laughs.

"Use the whole bottle!" Lori adds. They giggle and roll on the bed as Jody sprays.

Monique pulls an envelope out from under her back and looks at it. She turns to Lori.

"You ever gonna open these things?"

Jody hops on the bed with them, "I asked her the same thing earlier."

"Well, guess now is as good a time as any."

Lori slowly opens one envelope. She scans over the letter. Jody and Monique look at one another, shocked. They point at her and mouth to each other, "Is she okay?"

Lori sets that letter down and opens another envelope. She skims over the text. She picks up yet another, opens it and just looks at the paper, but doesn't even read it. Monique passes her the last envelope. She opens it and sets it down. She looks up at the girls.

"I can't do this. I can't choose."

"What do you mean," Jody asks.

"I thought that's what you wanted," Monique says. Jody's eyes widen and she elbows her.

"What?"

Lori shakes her head and smirks, "Eavesdropping again?"

"No, never," Monique lies.

"Too late now, dork. Thanks for giving it away," Jody turns to Lori. "We wanted to give you some privacy, but pipsqueak over here kept putting her ear to the door. I swore I was gonna die of laughter if you swung that door open and smacked her right in the face."

"Yeah, kinda like today in class."

All three went quiet.

Lori looks around the room. "How about we play a game?"

"You're supposed to be picking a school," Jody reminds her.

"Exactly. You guys pick for me."

"But, this is a big decision. You need to really think about it," Monique says.

Lori shakes her head, "I've never been allowed to make a decision in my life before, why start now?"

The girls all look at one another.

Lori puts all four letters in her hand. "Pick one."

CHAPTER 6: MEETING IN NEW YORK

"It's so nice to have you back in town again," Mrs. Clark smiles at the back of a large, chauffeured car.

Lori leans back and looks at her father. "How long are you here?" she asks.

"Until the end of the week." He replies, "Then off to Bangkok for a few weeks."

Lori nods, "I come back to the same continent ,and then you leave for another one. Nice." The car comes to a stop.

"I'll be back for your summer recital," Mr. Clark says.

"Performance," Lori corrects. "They were called recitals when I was like five, Dad."

"I liked those fluffy tutus. I loved them on all three of you girls."

Lori smiles.

"Your sisters each tour through New York during the summer. They hope to stop by," Mrs. Clark says.

"I know. I talked to Nadine yesterday."

The car comes to a stop. Lori opens the door and steps outside. She looks up at the building. The driver and her father get out of the car. Lori goes to the trunk, opens it, and pulls out a large rolling suitcase and small duffle bag. The driver rushes to help her with the luggage.

"Oh no, it's fine, thanks."

The driver looks to Mr. Clark.

"It's fine, thank you, Brandon."

The driver steps aside. Lori hugs Mr. Clark."

"Have a good trip, Dad."

He hugs her harder and kisses her head.

"Love you," Lori mumbles.

"Love you too."

Lori tosses the duffle bag over her shoulder and begins to roll the large suitcase. She walks toward the building.

"Point those toes my little princess." Lori looks back at him. He winks. She smiles, then turns and continues toward the building.

Inside the car Mrs. Clark smacks her lips together as she looks in a compact mirror. She closes her lipstick container and sets down the mirror, then exits the car.

"Now darling, I want you to..."

She sees Lori walking into the building.

"She just left?"

Mr. Clark watches Lori enter the building.

"But she didn't say goodbye."

"Maybe you should've gotten out of the car," he says sternly and walks to the front of the vehicle. "We're done here, Brandon."

The driver nods and opens the front passenger door for Mr. Clark. Mrs. Clark stares at him in amazement.

A long limousine pulls up behind their car. Miguel hops out of the car and opens the back door. Paige steps out.

"So, this is New York."

She coughs. "A bit more smoggy than Malibu."

Miguel looks around. "And taller."

Paige giggles.

Miguel goes to the trunk and removes several bags. "Anything else?"

Paige removes a piece of paper from her small clutch purse and then sets the purse on top of Miguel's load of luggage.

"That should be all. Follow me."

Paige commandingly struts toward a building. She looks at the paper; it reads: "800 Broadway." She reads the number on the building: "800."

Maybe there was a mistake.

The building is old and faded. Several tiles are broken and the entry way is littered with trash.

This can't be it.

A girl stands outside the building with her parents. Her mother holds a pair of ballet slippers in her hand. Paige approaches them.

"You aren't by chance here for the New York Company Ballet summer intensive are you?"

The girl jumps up, "Yes I am. Hi, I'm Charlene."

She extends her hand. "I'm super-excited. Are you super-excited? Don't you love the dorms?"

Expressionless, Paige responds, "So this isn't the school then?"

"No, these are the dorms, silly," Charlene replies. "They're really cool, you're gonna love it here."

Ummm, not loving it yet.

Out of the corner of her eye, Paige sees something scurry by.

- Was that a rat?

Her eyes widen. She turns to Miguel who struggles to balance all her bags.

Take me back to Malibu, pronto.

Miguel makes his way to the door and sets a couple bags down, so he can open the door. Paige enters. Miguel holds the door open with his foot, then grabs the bags he set down, and heads after her.

Paige walks into the lobby. A plump woman with glasses walks around with a clipboard and pencil in hand.

"The fashion institute dormitory is next door," she turns away, rudely.

Paige shakes her head, taken aback. She clears her throat, "I'm here for the NYCB intensive."

The woman spins back around. She looks Paige up and down and raises an eyebrow.

"Name?"

"Paige Ling."

The woman scans down her paper and finds Paige's name. She makes a checkmark beside her name.

"Room 213. Straight down the hall and to the right."

Paige nods, "Thank you." She starts down the hall. Miguel follows her.

"STOP!" The woman says.

Paige turns around.

"No men in the dorms."

Paige smiles, "Oh, he's just bringing my things to my room, then he'll be right back to his own apartment that my parents arranged for him in the city."

"No men."

"But he's just..."

The woman puts her hand in Paige's face.

"Say goodbye to the gentleman."

Paige looks at Miguel, then back at the woman.

"But, then who will take my bags to the room?" she asks.

The woman winks and points at Paige. "You've got two arms don't ya?" She waves at Miguel to leave.

Miguel looks at Paige. She looks at him, then nods and lowers her eyes.

"If you need me Miss Paige, you know where I am," he says.

She half-smiles, "Thanks, Miguel."

Miguel walks out of the building. The doors push in a gush of air which hits Paige's back. She shivers.

"Better get to it if you want to choose a bed. One of your roommates has already checked in."

Paige looks at her mountain of bags.

"How many roommates do I have?" she questions.

"Three."

Paige's jaw drops.

"I hope they're mini- suites or none of our things will fit in."

The woman chuckles, "Oh yeah, mini -suites alright."

Paige grabs a couple of bags and starts to throw them over her shoulder; the bags are larger than she is.

She starts down the hall.

The woman chuckles again, "Mini- suites! Never heard that one before."

* * * * * * * * * * * * * * * * * *

Kelsi walks out of JFK Airport. Dressed in cut off jean shorts, a spaghetti strap top and heeled flip flops, she pulls her rhinestone-covered luggage to the curb and looks around.

Kelsi puts two fingers in her mouth and whistles. With sunglasses on her head and a long ponytail streaming down her back, she looks like a movie star. Several guys turn their heads and stare at her.

"Taxi!" She yells.

Three taxis pull up at the same time.

And people say it's hard to get a cab here.

One taxi driver gets out and grabs her luggage. She gets into the car and it speeds off.

Kelsi looks out the window at the large buildings.

Wow! They don't build them this tall at home.

She continues to look around, shifting from one window to another.

The taxi driver looks in his rear view mirror. "Not from here?"

"No. Is it that obvious?" She replies.

"Yep, you look like a Barbie doll. Probably from LA, huh?" he snickers.

Kelsi raises an eyebrow.

Ughh, you're like older than my dad. Gross!

The car comes to a stop. Kelsi looks out the window at gridlocked traffic. She looks at her watch.

I am gonna be so late.

"How far is the ballet school from here?" she asks.

"'Bout six blocks."

"Six blocks? That's it? I walk six blocks just from the closest parking to the Promenade." She grabs her bedazzled bag. "I'll get out here," she says.

"You sure?" he asks.

"Yeah, I think I can handle it," she says confidently.

The taxi driver pops the trunk but remains in the car. Kelsi gets out and grabs her bags. She looks for the sidewalk and struts over rolling her luggage. "I can do this."

The taxi driver shakes his head and laughs, "Good luck."

* * * * * * * * * * * * * * * * * *

Kelsi trudges into the dorm building, body hunched over. She plops down on one of the bags. Beads of sweat run down her face and create mascara lines across her cheeks.

"Six blocks?" she mutters.

The woman with the clipboard looks at her, confused.

Six blocks, my butt. More like six miles.

"Are you here for the ballet school?" the woman questions.

Kelsi breathes heavily and nods from her sprawled out position on the floor.

"Name?"

"Kelsi. Kelsi Little."

The woman scans down the page. "Ah there you are. Room 213. Two of your roommates have already checked in. Just waiting on one more."

Kelsi struggles to get up. She wipes away the beads of sweat on her forehead.

"Are all blocks in New York that long?"

"In the city," she nods, "but don't worry, you won't have to do too much of that."

She pats her back. "Go meet your roommates."

Kelsi's forehead scrunches up.

"Nervous?" the woman asks.

Kelsi nods.

"Don't be. Have confidence when you walk in and act like you own the place. Do the same in class and you'll be fine. You have to believe in yourself, right?"

Kelsi nods. She takes a deep breath. Her smile appears.

I can do this.

"Thanks."

Kelsi heads down the hall with her luggage.

The woman watches her and smirks. "That one's gonna have some trouble," she mutters to herself.

* * * * * * * * * * * * * * * * * * *

Lori carefully removes items from her luggage, refolds them and sets them in a set of drawers. Paige enters and watches from the doorway. Lori doesn't notice her. Every crease on her clothing is perfect. She brushes her hand across each folded garment to smooth out any imperfections.

"Can you do mine next?"

Paige rolls a single suitcase in. Lori sees the large stack of luggage behind her in the doorway.

"Where's that all going?" she asks.

Paige looks back at it. "I'm sure you can be accommodating when you see the loads of Dolce and Gabanna inside."

Paige plops her rolling suitcase down. She looks around at the small room. There are two sets of bunk beds, two large dressers, a door leading to a bathroom and an empty space in the middle. She looks at both sets of bunk beds.

"I'll take that one," Paige points at the bunk bed where Lori folds her clothes.

"I've got bottom, so you can have top."

Paige looks confused, "But I just said I wanted that one."

"Yeah, and I claimed the bottom. First come, first serve."

Lori continues to fold her clothes and put them away.

"But I want that one. You can have the other one." Paige nods to the other bed. "This bed is facing the correct way for my feng shui."

"You've never done this before, have you?"

"Oh, I do feng shui all the time. My trainer suggested it would help center my core."

Lori laughs, "And I thought I was spoiled." She shakes her head. "What I meant was ballet; you've never done a summer intensive have you?"

Paige shakes her head. "I've only done independent training and company performances. My parents thought this would widen my perspective."

"Well, my parents thought shipping me off for ballet boarding school the last five years would be good for my global perspective too. I'm a pro at this."

Paige is still confused.

"These bunks mean there are more people coming, you have to choose your bed now, or you'll be stuck with whatever's left."

"There are more girls staying here? I thought the lady was kidding."

"Yeah. Four beds. Four people. I suggest the bottom bunk. It's easier to get in and out of bed, plus you won't have to worry about stepping on someone, just getting stepped on."

Paige looks at the other bunk. She takes a deep breath.

"Alright, bottom bunk it is."

Paige begins to open her bag. A pile of designer clothes are inside. Lori notices the designer labels and price tags still attached.

"You are definitely more spoiled than me. I didn't think that was possible." Lori stands beside Paige and stares at the clothes.

"May I?" she asks.

Paige nods. "Absolutely."

Lori reaches down and touches the silk clothes then pulls back her hand quickly.

"Thanks, that was fun."

"You can wear them you know," Paige says.

Lori's eyes widen, "Really?"

I can wear Dolce and Gabanna!

"No, I can't. These are brand new. You haven't even worn them it wouldn't be right."

"It's okay. Trust me. My parents buy me clothes as their way of not being around and trying to make it okay. They basically buy me off."

"Wow, upfront."

"It's a new thing I'm trying," Paige responds.

"I think we might just get along."

Paige smiles and extends her hand. "Paige Ling," she curtsies, "Nice to meet you."

"Lori Clark," she does a deep curtsy, "the pleasure is all mine."

The girls both start to giggle.

"211, 212, 213. Ah, here it is.", comes from the hall.

Both girls turn to the doorway.

Kelsi trudges in, her hair a mess and mascara still running down her face.

Confidence.

Paige and Lori look at her, surprised.

"213?"

They both nod.

"Good." She drags her bags in and drops them beside Paige's bunk.

"Uh, that's taken."

"Fine," Kelsi replies as she lifts her chin and struts to the other side of the room. She turns back and looks at the girls.

"Top," Lori points to the top bunk.

"Cool," Kelsi turns away and tosses a duffle bag up onto the top bunk. Facing away from them she takes a deep breath. Tears well in her eyes. She bites her lip and swallows hard then spins around, trying hard to be tough.

"So, I'm Kelsi, I dance for LBT Dance Company and have won practically every award in the competition circuit for the past three years in a row. And ,yes, I am the current Junior Miss Showstopper." She props her hip out and poses.

Confidence.

Kelsi smiles proudly, "And you are?"

The girls look at one another. Lori nods to Paige.

"Paige Ling."

She looks to Lori.

"Lori Clark. Royal Academy of Ballet." She says in a perfect British accent. Paige turns and stares at her.

"You're from England?" Kelsi asks.

"Yes, dear. Leeds to be exact." The accent continues. Paige raises an eyebrow.

"Cool," Kelsi says excited, but not wanting to seem overly impressed, she adds, "I mean, it's too cold there. Royal pain."

"Pity, England is lovely," Lori winks at Paige.

"Yeah, whatever," Kelsi turns and ignores them.

Keep it together Kels. Keep it together.

She pulls a compact out of her bag and flips open the mirror to look at herself. Kelsi's eyes widen as she sees the black streaks down her cheeks and messy hair. She closes the compact and quickly makes her way into the bathroom.

Paige and Lori looks at each other. Paige lips to Lori, "England?"

Lori smiles. "It's not a complete lie."

They smirk at one another then look at the empty bed.

"Think we'll get another one of those?" She nods to the bathroom.

Lori shrugs her shoulders.

Paige sighs. Lori laughs.

"Gotta love summer ballet intensives."

CHAPTER 7: TAP

Gisela and a bunch of other dancers, all clap. Gisela smiles as she grabs her bag. Derek grabs his bag and drinks from a sports bottle.

"See you tomorrow, Zel?"

"You know it," she replies.

Alan stands by the door and greets students as they leave.

Gisela makes her way to the door.

"See you in class tomorrow. Be fresh for the first day of your tap intensive."

Gisela smiles widely.

"Wouldn't miss it for the world."

Excited, she skips out of the room.

A moment later, Gisela is on the streets of New York dancing around. She excitedly jumps up and clicks her heels together.

A whole summer of tap. Doesn't get any better than this!

She skips down the street like a little girl.

* * * * * * * * * * * * * * * * * * *

Gisela talks on the phone and paces around her pink ballet-painted bedroom. Posters of Fred Astaire, Gregory Hines and Bojangles Robinson cover framed photos of ballerinas.

"I know, huh?"

She stares at a poster of Fred Astaire dancing with a coat rack.

"I can't wait! It's gonna be so much fun!"

She does a double-time step as she talks on the phone.

"Oh it's easy. So I get dressed like I'm going to ballet class right? Bun, tights, the whole getup."

She picks up a new pair of ballet slippers on her bed and tosses them on the floor.

"I'll leave like I'm going to NYCB and then take the subway to tap instead. It's a totally brilliant plan."

Gisela paces and listens for a moment.

"No, she'll never even think that. My mom trusts me. She just wants me to be the little ballerina she was, and I'm just not."

Gisela plops down on her bed and rolls onto her stomach.

"I mean, yeah, I have that. Ballet's easy. But it's not like tap. It's like the music comes on and the rhythm and beat gets going and I just can't stop. It's like it's part of me or something. I don't know. I can't really explain it."

Gisela rolls on her back and taps her feet in the air.

"Yeah, I'll totally be there."

There's a knock at the door.

"Zel, dinner's ready!" her mother calls through the door.

Gisela puts the phone to her chest, "Be there in a minute."

She puts the phone back to her ear, "Gotta go, dinner time, but I'll see you tomorrow, kay?"

Gisela grins ear to ear.

"I know, can't wait!"

She hangs up the phone and rolls off her bed.

* * * * * * * * * * * * * * * * * *

A small dinner table is set with three place settings. Gisela, her mom, and father, Giancarlo, all eat salad.

"Picked out the perfect leotard for your premiere yet?" Giancarlo asks.

"Dad, it's just class."

"The first day. You want to make a good impression," he replies.

"The first day of the rest of your life, hopefully," Tatiana adds. "This could be a very big step for you. Intensive student this year, company member down the line, and eventually prima ballerina."

"You could be just like your mom."

"No, you could be better. I wish I'd had that turn-out at your age."

Gisela continues to look down and eat her salad.

"Should I tell her or would you like to?" Giancarlo asks Tatiana.

Gisela looks up.

"Tell me what?" she asks.

"Well honey…." Tatiana starts.

"We think it would be best if you stayed in the dorms this summer."

Giancarlo finishes.

"But, we only live twenty minutes away."

"Yes, well, we think it would be better for you. Enable you to focus more on your class time and get in extra stretch," Tatiana says.

"But I don't want to live in the dorms. I want to stay here. I want to live right here. With you."

"We're going to Europe for the summer so we can't do that," Giancarlo states.

"Wait, Europe?" her eyes dart back and forth between the two. "When did this come up?"

"Just the other day, sweetie pie." Tatiana says.

"And you decide to tell me this the night before classes start?"

I have tap in the morning.

"We meant to tell you sooner but with the social on Tuesday and that gallery event the other night time just slipped right on by," Giancarlo says.

"We've arranged a dorm-living situation for you. It's with three other girls so you'll have plenty of company. I bet you'll all be best friends by Monday even. Oh, honey, you're going to have so much fun. I remember my first intensive," Tatiana stares off lost in a dream. "Best summer of my life." She looks to Giancarlo, "Beside the summer I met you." She grabs his hand and smiles.

Vomit. Come on now. Gross!

Gisela rolls her eyes, "Great."

She looks down at her plate and mopes, "Can I be excused?"

"Yes darling. And go ahead and pack. We're supposed to take you there tonight before dark."

Are you serious?

Gisela looks over at a window. The sun is setting.

"Thanks for the warning."

She turns and stomps off to her room.

* * * * * * * * * * * * * * * * * *

Phone against her ear, Gisela places dance clothes and shoes into a small rolling suitcase.

"And what am I supposed to do now? I had it all figured out until they screwed everything up."

She pulls down a poster of Bojangles.

"Sorry, Bo, but you gotta go."

Under the Bojangles print is a photo of a Degas ballerina.

"I'll figure something out," she says into the phone then hangs up.

Gisela falls back on her bed and looks up at the ceiling.

"But I don't want to be a ballerina."

"Zel, you packed?" Her mother calls from the hallway.

"Almost," Gisela yells back.

Almost never.

* * * * * * * * * * * * * * * * *

Tatiana drives. Gisela looks at her mother, then down at her squiggling toes. Her fingers tap each other nervously.

"Mom…" she starts.

Tatiana looks at her, ready to listen, then turns and looks ahead at the road.

"I uh…I know you're all into the ballet and stuff, and don't get me wrong, I love it, too, but there's this tap intensive…"

Tatiana sighs, "We've talked about this before."

"Not really."

Tatiana looks at her questionably. "What do you mean?"

"Well, don't get mad, but I went to an audition for the intensive and I got in."

"You what?!?"

"You said you wouldn't get mad."

"No, I didn't."

"Okay, maybe I threw that part in."

Gisela flashes a cheesy fake smile.

"Please mom, pretty, pretty, please," she begs.

Tatiana shakes her head. "Absolutely not."

"Can't you even just consider it?"

"Sure."

Gisela sits up. Her face brightens.

"Really?"

"Uh huh," Tatiana replies, "Considering…uh, still no."

Gisela sinks back into her seat.

This sucks.

* * * * * * * * * * * * * * * * *

Tatiana speaks with the woman in the lobby. She gives her a hug.

"It's really great seeing you Ms. Korpova…"

"Mrs. Palente," Tatiana corrects.

"Yes, beg my pardon. I just always still think of you as the famous Korpova."

Tatiana smiles gently.

"But you really must be going. It's lights out for the girls in a few minutes." The woman continues.

"I understand."

Tatiana turns to Gisela. She places her hands on her daughter's beautiful face.

"You are going to be wonderful. You have a heart of gold and the passion of a dancer."

She hugs her and whispers in her ear, "I am so proud of you." She takes a step back and waves softly, "Love you, Zel Bel." She blows a kiss then leaves through the front doors.

* * * * * * * * * * * * * * * * * *

Paige, Lori and Kelsi all lie in their beds and face the center of the room.

"I wonder if tomorrow will be like hell week," Kelsi says.

"What do you mean?" Paige asks.

"You know, like football players have a really hard week where they separate the serious people from the goofs."

"I don't think so," Lori says in her British accent.

All of a sudden the door swings open. Gisela steps inside.

"Hi, girls, I'm you're number four."

"Lights out!" The woman down the hall yells.

The lights turn off.

CHAPTER 8: ROOMMATES

Paige opens her eyes and looks around at the small room. Across from her, Lori is just waking up. Gisela moves around on the top bunk and texts on her cell phone.

"Yeah, I'll be there. No worries. I'll sneak out at lunch," she texts.

Paige gets out of bed and begins a series of stretches. She rolls her neck and pushes over her arches. Lori sits up.

"We have a two hour barre followed by a stretch class, you know?" she says.

"Yes, but I have a routine. My trainer wouldn't want me to ruin all his work."

"Ballet schmallet," Gisela says as she hops down from the top. "It's all pointed toes and turn-out. Ace that and you're fine."

"And you are?" Lori asks.

"Zel."

"Zel? That's different. Do you have a last name, Zel?" Lori continues.

"Palente." Zel texts again on her cell phone.

"Palente?" Paige asks. "As in the Palente venture capitalist family?"

Lori scrunches up her face.

"What?"

"Yeah, that's my dad and grandpa's thing," Gisela replies. "My mom was a ballerina."

"Oh, so it's in your blood. Me, too, my sisters are both company members. Well, one was just promoted to soloist. Lot of pressure. Everyone expects me to better than them for some reason. Ah, the trials of being a ballerina."

"I'm not a ballerina. I'm a tap dancer," mutters Zel.

"Then why are you here?" Paige asks.

"I won't be," Gisela replies.

Lori and Paige look at each other, confused.

"If you don't see me after lunch, just assume I got the flu and had to go home," she winks. "Got it there, London Tipton?"

Paige scowls, "Paige. My name is Paige."

"Sorry, I don't mean to be rude... it's just I won't be here long so there's no real point in getting all buddy, buddy cause like I said, I'll be gone by lunch. I just have to stay long enough for my parents to leave the country, thenI'll be in the clear."

Gisela pulls on a pair of pink tights.

"Couple hours of this and I'll be free."

"Where are you going?" Paige asks.

Lori brushes her long hair.

"Tap intensive," Gisela replies. "I'll go there during the day, then just go home at night. No one has to know. When my parents call, I'll just tell them what a great day I had at ballet and how much my fouetté turns are improving. Blah, blah, blah. Everyone's happy."

"Wow. Sounds like you have it all figured out." Lori says.

Lori quickly twists her hair back and pins it into a perfect bun. Paige watches amazed, and hands her a brush.

"Do mine?"

Lori laughs, "Do you have a personal hairstylist at home too?"

"Sort of," Paige mumbles.

She sits on the edge of the bed. Lori sits behind her and brushes her hair.

Gisela pulls on her leotard. "So you're all really into ballet then, right?"

Paige nods. "Yep," Lori answers. "Don't move your head." She continues to brush Paige's hair. "Why did you even audition if you didn't want to come?"

"Mom made me." Gisela says, "I dance here, so it's not a big deal or anything. Audition was just like another class."

"You dance here?" Kelsi says from the bathroom. She appears in the doorway. "I am so jealous."

The girls all stare at Kelsi. She wears high-cut, black booty shorts over pink tights and a black sports bra. Her eyes are covered with sparkly eye shadow and false eyelashes. Her hair is slicked back into two buns like ponytails, each complete with a layer of sparkles.

The girls continue to stare at her, all in a state of shock.

"You might..." Lori starts in her British accent.

"What are you all looking at? Maybe if you get up earlier tomorrow, you can look as good as I do," Kelsi cuts her off and slams the bathroom door closed.

"Should we…." Lori starts and points toward the bathroom.

"Nah," Gisela shakes her head.

Lori twirls Paige's hair and spins it into a bun on her head. She places couple bobby pins in place.

"All done," Lori says.

Paige shakes her head side to side.

"That was so fast," Paige looks in a small mirror on the dresser. "You're amazing."

"Thanks, that's what several years of boarding school will do for you."

Lori and Paige quickly dress.

Kelsi pushes the bathroom door open, "Let's rock this."

She struts out, now donning red lipstick, a small bag draped over her arm. She walks past the girls and right out the door into the hallway.

Paige massages her toes, "Should I pack my pointe shoes?"

"Pointe's   after   lunch." Lori runs her finger down the schedule. "She's right, not until 2. I'm gonna post this so we can all look at it, okay?"

Lori takes the schedule and tapes it to the wall beside the door.

"Everyone ready?" Gisela asks.

Paige and Lori nod. They all head out the door. Gisela does as well, and then closes the door.

* * * * * * * * * * * * * * * * * * *

"Welcome to the New York Company Ballet Summer Intensive," Phillipe Morin says. The room of young ballet dancers erupts in polite applause.

"You were the best at each of your studios, that's why you auditioned. You were amongst the best when we saw you, but let me tell you, that doesn't mean you were the best."

Paige frowns. Gisela looks around at the other dancers, ignoring Phillipe's message.

"We turned away dancers better than many of you."

Huh? Lori thinks.

"You're here because we saw something in you we liked. We saw a spark. Potential."

Kelsi stands up tall; a smile comes across her face.

"Your passion, your transparency when you dance, your sheer strength."

Phillipe scans the room and makes eye contact with everyone.

"You used to be a big fish in a small pond. Now you're a small fish in a

a built-in filtration system used to get rid of
lsi. She feels his stare piercing her skin.
ie for?
mprove your technique. Secondly, it's to nab one of
round training program. Do that, and you have a
ina. Don't, and you can kiss your chances goodbye."
es drop. One girl is on the verge of tears. She wipes
her eyes.

Phillipe chuckles, "Just kidding."

There's a collective sigh.

"But getting a spot will definitely improve your chance, that's for sure."

Gisela casually chews on a piece of gum. She stops chewing each time Phillipe looks her way.

"In order to increase our success rate and give our students the best chance possible, we have created a strict code of conduct. The following are not guidelines, they are concrete rules."

Yeah, yeah, whatever, Phillipe. Let's get on with this.

"The first is dress code."

He starts to walk over to Kelsi.

"Here is the perfect example…"

He motions toward Kelsi. She places her hands on her hips and poses, a full proud smile which lights up the room."

"….of what not to do."

She continues to smile.

"This is atrocious."

Her smile fades.

"What's your name?"

Phillipe glares at her. She cowers and swallows hard.

"Kelsi Little."

"Kelsi Little. That outfit. Is that how you dance for ballet?"

Paige elbows Lori. Both girls watch and try to hide their growing smiles.

Kelsi shakes her head, "yes."

"It is?" Phillipe asks.

Kelsi shakes her head, "no."

"It isn't?" he questions, puzzled.

"No sir, it is, but it isn't how I will for here," Kelsi stammers out.

"Do you not take this ballet seriously?" he asks.

"No. I…"

"No?"

"No. No. That's not…I mean…" She tries to start again.

"If it's not, then…"

"It is. I want to be here. I take it seriously. I just didn't know!" she yells. The room falls silent.

Phillipe walks around Kelsi, hands behind his back, inspecting her attire. He stops in front of her face.

"Dress code. Pink tights, black leotard, hair in a bun, slicked back. No rhinestones or sparkles, no colored hair bands, no eye make-up, no jewelry. No nail polish. Simple, clean, professional."

Kelsi tremors and shakes.

"Any questions?"

Kelsi's eyes plead to speak. Phillipe raises an eyebrow.

Should I ask? Oh God, what if he kicks me out.

Kelsi timidly raises her arm up, just above her shoulder.

"Yes?" Phillipe asks.

"Parted or smooth?" Kelsi says, her voice quivers.

"Parted or smooth what?"

Kelsi's eyes turn up toward the top of her head.

"Hair. Buns. Parted or smooth?"

She closes her eyes waiting for a response.

Here it comes. He's going to say it. He's going to...

Phillipe starts to laugh. Kelsi opens an eye. Phillipe stands before her and continues to laugh. Kelsi is puzzled.

What?

Phillipe's laugh becomes louder, like a howl.

What is so funny?

Paige and Lori look at one another. Lori leans into Paige and whispers, "I think he might be a little crazy." Paige nods. "I think you're right."

Phillipe stops laughing instantly and steps back staring directly in Kelsi's face.

"Go and change now. Get to code or get out. Next time you come to class inappropriately dressed, it will be your last class here. Understand?"

Kelsi nods, tears in her eyes. Phillipe takes a couple steps back.

"Go on. Get moving and change." He motions for her to leave. Kelsi turns and heads for the door.

Phillipe claps his hands together. "On with it."

A small Dutch woman moves into the center of the room.

"To the barre." She says, "Let's begin today with plies in all five, port de bras around and plie sou sou."

Gisela looks up at the clock. It reads "9:45 am."

Still an hour and a half to get there.

The woman turns to the pianist. "3/4 time please." The pianist begins to play. All the girls start the plie sequence in first position.

* * * * * * * * * * * * * * * * *

A line of dancers wraps down the hallway into a small room of the building. Inside the room, Paige steps up on the scale. A woman stands beside her with a clipboard and pencil in hand. She adjusts the scale.

"87." The nutritionist says, "That gives you a BMI of under 16. Perfect for a ballerina."

Paige smiles proudly.

"How many hours of physical activity a week are customary for you?"

"22."

"I suggest increasing your carb intake, because you'll be having more hours while you're here and your body could use the extra energy. Energy bars, whole wheat pasta, fruit."

She hands Paige a sheet of paper, "This is just a list of more suggested snacks. Do you have any issues you'd like to ask about?"

Issues? Yes.

"Issues?" Paige asks.

"Yeah, things you want to talk about regarding food or exercise for body issues."

Why is she asking me this? How could she know…no, there's no way. She couldn't.

"No."

The nutritionist smiles, "Keep up the good work, young lady. Whatever you're doing is working."

"Thanks."

Paige leaves the room and walks into the hall past the others waiting in line.

Gisela stands in line and taps her toes. Kelsi is behind her and dressed in a conservative black leotard with her hair slicked back in a bun.

"You tap?"

Gisela looks down at her toes moving.

"Kinda a habit," she replies.

"I take tap too," Kelsi says. "It's super fun."

Super fun? Where is this girl from?

"I won with my tap solo last season." Kelsi continues, "The judges loved it."

"I'm sure they did," Gisela says sarcastically.

"Do you tap in competition?"

"Nope."

"Ah, you should. It's a lot of fun."

"My mom won't let me. She hardly ever even lets me leave here as it is."

"She's already keeping tabs on you? But it's just the first day," Kelsi says, astonished.

"This is where I dance. Like, all the time. I dance at the New York Company Ballet," Gisela explains.

"You're from here?"

"Yep. Native New Yorker."

"You're so lucky."

Gisela rolls her eyes, "Yeah, whatever."

"Do they always do that much barre, my ankles are already killing me."

"Two hours every day." Gisela says. "How'd you like the stretch class?"

"Pretty killer."

Gisela grins and looks at the clock on her cell phone.

"Expecting a call?"

Gisela shakes her head, "Can't wait for lunch."

"I know. I'm starving," Kelsi rubs her stomach. "I hope they have something good. I'm craving fried chicken and fries right now." She smiles at the thought of chicken and fries.

Gisela giggles.

"Good luck with that one."

Lori walks out of the nutritionist's office. She stops and looks at Gisela.

"They told me I was fat." She looks down at her body. "I'm not fat am I?"

Kelsi looks at her, shocked.

"What happened to the accent?"

Gisela and Lori both look at her puzzled and then it dawns on them. Lori was faking an accent the night before.

"But...but you..."

Lori cracks a smile. She starts to laugh.

"Didn't you say you were from England?" Kelsi questions.

"I danced there. I'm from the States."

"Oh."

"Gotta run. Off to costume fittings. Yippee. More people who will tell me I'm fat." She puts on a thick accent, "Sorry to have messed with you...pip pip, cheerio."

Lori waves like the queen and walks down the hall, giggling.

Kelsi watches her walk away.

"She's not fat. She's perfect."

"In the real world," Gisela responds.

Kelsi looks down at her own body. She sucks in her non-existent stomach.

Gisela watches her with a half-smile.

Ah, newbies crack me up.

* * * * * * * * * * * * * * * * * *

Bolts of fabric and spools of thread fill the cabinet covered walls of a small sewing room. Several of the girls stand in the middle, a few stand with their arms spread out as a woman adjusts a tape measure and writes down numbers.

Lori grabs her water bottle and takes a sip.

"Now, don't change size by August."

"I was just told to lose five pounds," Lori says.

"Do, and you'll be swimming in your costume ten weeks from now," the seamstress replies.

I need lunch.

* * * * * * * * * * * * * * * * * *

A buffet station is filled with lettuce, salad toppings, and grilled chicken. Kelsi pushes her tray along the station. Her plate is empty. She looks around. Several girls sit at tables and eat their salad happily. A woman refills the bowl of beets.

"Excuse me. Where are the other selections?" Kelsi asks.

"I'm sorry?"

"The other foods. You know, chicken, fries, pizza, soup. Where are they?"

The woman frowns, "We don't have any."

"Okay, thanks."

Kelsi uses tongs to fill her plate with lettuce. She begins to add toppings. She gets to the end of the buffet section and sees a stack of lemons and a spray bottle of water.

Where's the 'ranch'?

She looks around for salad dressing.

Bleu cheese, where are you?

Another girl comes up behind her.

"Scuse me." She leans across Kelsi and grabs the spray bottle. She squirts her place of lettuce a few times then sets the bottle back down and walks off to a table. Another girl approaches the end of the buffet station.

"Where is the dressing?" Kelsi asks.

"Right there."

The girl points to the lemon.

"That's it? No ranch, no bleu cheese, and no thousand island?"

The girl squeezes the lemon over her salad.

"Too many calories," the girl replies.

Kelsi sighs, and squeezes the lemon over her salad plate.

At a table, Paige and Lori nibble on salad together.

"So, what do you think of the new girl?" Paige asks.

"Seems nice enough. That Miley Cyrus wannabe is something else though. She actually thought I was British," Lori jokes.

* * * * * * * * * * * * * * * * *

Gisela peeks out of a room and looks down the hallway. She looks left, then right, no one is in sight. She hops into the hallway and jogs, looking behind her as she runs with a small bag over her arm. She starts to turn a corner and looks back.

"Gisela," A friendly voice says.

Gisela turns and sees Naomi Briana, the pas de deux teacher.

"Hi, Naomi," Gisela replies shyly.

"Your mother phoned and told me you'd be here. She's so excited."

"Yes, aren't we all?" Gisela lies.

"I'm sad you won't be in my class this summer. I'm sure you'll be back next summer with the older advanced students."

"We'll see," Gisela shrugs.

Not if I have anything to do with it.

Naomi smiles at her.

"Well, it was really good to see. I gotta go…I mean you probably have other things to do," Gisela tries to cover.

"Actually, I'm completely free."

Of course you are.

"Walk with me."

Naomi starts back down the hall toward the ballet school classes. Gisela looks down the hall the other way and reaches toward the door.

Noooooo!

She turns around and starts to walk with Naomi.

"I'm not supposed to tell you this. But your mom was kinda worried about you. Is there anything you want to talk about?" Naomi asks.

Going to tap.

Gisela shakes her head.

"Boys, school…" Naomi continues.

Tap intensive…

"Nothing at all?"

Gisela shakes her head. "Nothing bothering me that I can think of."

They get to the end of a hallway with a couple open doors. In one a group of male and female ballet dancers stretch independently.

"Alright, well if you ever need someone, I'm here," Naomi says with a soft smile.

"Thanks," Gisela smiles.

Thanks you just took up all my time to escape! Witch!

Naomi half-waves and enters the classroom where the dancers stretch. The students all jump to their feet when they see her.

Gisela pulls her cell phone out of her bag. The time reads "12:56."

Shoot. Class starts in four minutes. Thanks, Naomi,...for wasting my time.

She shakes her head. "What do I say?" she says to herself.

Her eyes light up. She starts to dial numbers on the phone then holds it up to her ear.

"Hello? Hi, this is Gisela Palente. I sorry I'm won't be able to make it today, there was a family emergency...oh, thank you...yes, everything will be fine...I'll be there tomorrow...thanks...bye."

She closes the phone, her eyes beam with determination.

"Tomorrow," she mutters to herself.

* * * * * * * * * * * * * * * * * * *

During the leaps and turns class, Kelsi shines with her high jumps and fast spinning ability. Gisela dances lackadaisically, but her technique is flawless. Paige does the minimum turns, but her natural turnout leaves others drooling. Lori struggles to keep up with the jumps. Her jetés are lower than the others and her sautés barely get off the ground.

* * * * * * * * * * * * * * * * * * *

In pointe class the students perform a combination of relevés and elevés. Phillipe and the Russian woman from auditions, walk around and critique the girls.

Lori does better on pointe, but she is still not completely concentrated. The Russian woman pokes her in the ribs.

"Under."

Lori sucks in more, exposing her ribs through the leotard and rotating her hips outward.

Paige holds a second position eleve effortlessly.

"Excellent balance," Phillipe comments.

Gisela pushes over her toes dangerously hard, as if doing toe taps.

"Relax." The Russian woman says, "You're already there."

Kelsi thinks hard about her technique and tries to balance on pointe, but slips off a few times.

"Over the center of the toes. You're curling in to the big

toe," Phillipe tells her. He readjusts her right foot and pushes it to right. "Here. You feel that?"

Kelsi nods.

"That's where you want to be at all times. Otherwise you might roll your ankle," he continues.

"Aghhhh!" A scream is let out behind them.

Phillipe turns around to see a willowy dancer roll her ankle and fall to the ground. Phillipe sighs. He turns to Kelsi, "See what I mean."

Kelsi watches in horror as the poor girl wriggles in pain on the floor. The Russian woman kneels beside her. She touches the girl's ankle and gently squeezes a few spots.

"Here?"

The girl breathes heavily. The Russian woman moves her fingers on the ankle.

"Here?"

The girl cringes and cries. The Russian woman looks up at Phillipe who now stands over them. She nods.

"Alright, dear. We're going to send you to the hospital because we think you might have a broken ankle."

The girl cries and clutches her ankle in pain.

"Go with her, please."

The Russian woman nods and helps her to her feet. A couple of men standing by the doorway come over, pick up the girl and carry her away.

"Have Natalie call the first person on the wait list, and see if we can get them here tomorrow," Phillipe tells the Russian woman. She nods and leaves.

Phillipe turns around; the girls stare with wide eyes.

"And that's what happens when you're not focused. Let this be a lesson to you all. One day you're in, and the next…you're out."

Kelsi gulps hard.

Uh, oh.

CHAPTER 9: TROUBLE

Gisela lies in bed. There's the sound of movement and girls getting ready in the room. She opens her eyes and sees Kelsi and Lori putting on their shoes.

"Should we wake her?" Kelsi asks.

"I think so," Lori says.

Gisela quickly closes her eyes and pretends to be asleep. Kelsi steps on the bottom bunk and peeks over at Gisela. She gently shakes her.

"Time to get up, sleepyhead."

Gisela rolls over and acts groggy.

"Ah, I don't wanna get up," she mumbles.

"Class starts in fifteen minutes, you have to." Kelsi is face to face with her.

"I don't feel so good."

Kelsi moves her head back.

"I think I might puke," Gisela says.

Gisela pretends to gag and looks like she might throw up. She covers her mouth. Kelsi jumps back off the bed.

"Uh... maybe you should stay here today," she says.

"But, I don't want to miss class," Gisela moans.

"We'll tell the instructors you're not feeling well," Lori says. "Ready to go?" She looks at Kelsi, who nods.

Lori knocks on the bathroom door. "We're taking off, Paige. Ready?"

"Go without me. I'll catch up!" she yells from behind the door.

"Hope you feel better," Kelsi says.

Gisela sticks her thumb up over the edge of her bed. Kelsi and Lori head out.

Gisela breathes a sigh of relief. She gets down from the top bunk and grabs her tap shoes.

The bathroom door opens and Paige walks out. Gisela hides her tap shoes behind her back. Paige pulls her hair back and slicks it into a ponytail. "Not feeling well?" she asks.

"No, not at all," Gisela pretends.

Leave, leave, leave.

"In fact, I think I might have to…"

She rushes into the bathroom and closes the door. Paige uses bobby pins to turn her ponytail into a bun then covers it with a thin hairnet.

Gisela looks around the bathroom, frantic. She finds a cup half-filled with water. She lifts the toilet seat, makes a gagging sound and starts to pour the water in.

"Aghhhh, blahhhhhhhhhh," she moans as she looks at the door.

Paige sucks in her stomach and looks at her waist in a small mirror on the dresser.

Too much soup last night.

She releases her stomach which returns to a flat, six-pack abs, then sifts through her bag for something. Paige removes a small paper bag. She opens the bag and pulls the handles of a plastic bag which serves as lining over the outside of the paper bag. Gisela continues to pretend to throw up in the bathroom.

"Blahhhh!"

Paige pulls a plastic surgical glove from her bag. She carefully puts it on her right hand. She holds the bag with her left hand then sticks a finger on her gloved hand down her throat. She gags for a second, a dry heave, and then a little puke escapes and falls into the bag.

Gisela continues to pretend to throw up. Her throat becomes dry and she coughs.

She hears the sound of throwing up coming from the room. She pauses, unsure of what she hears.

"Blah, blah…"

Giselaopens the door quickly. Paige turns and shakes her glove off into the paper bag. She wipes her mouth and busies herself crumpling the bag and trying to casually throw it into her dance bag.

"Paige? It is Paige, right?"

"You don't know my name by now? We're roommates."

"It's only the second day, and honestly, I didn't even think I'd be here this long. Sorry. But are you…are you okay?" Gisela asks.

"I'm fine. I just have a nervous stomach. I get sick when I'm under pressure and being here just has me stressed to be perfect. It'll go away. It's happened before, honest."

Gisela raises an eyebrow.

That's what my mom used to say, too.

"You sure?" She asks.

"Fine." Paige stares at her, eyes pleading to believe her lie.

Gisela nods, "Okay."

"But please don't tell anyone. I don't want them to think I'm weak or get in trouble or anything."

Gisela smiles closed-lipped. "Sure. No worries."

She starts to close the door then stops.

"But if you ever do need anything, let me know."

"Thanks, Zel."

Gisela closes the door. Paige lets out a deep breath. She grabs her dance bag and leaves the room. A large trash bin is in the hall. She drops the paper bag in as she passes it.

Gisela presses her back against the bathroom door and leans her head back on it.

What do I do?

She looks down at her the time on her cell phone.

Get to class! I have to make it today!

She opens the bathroom door, takes off her pajama top to reveal a sports bra, throws on a shirt and heads out the door. She opens the door again and grabs a pair of shoes.

"Almost forgot."

* * * * * * * * * * * * * * * * * *

Gisela escapes out the front of the building.

Freedom!

Gisela rushes to the subway station entrance and jogs down the stairs as fast as she can. Token in hand, she slips it into the slot and presses through the divider. She rushes over to her waiting section and looks at her cell phone.

Plenty of time.

She happily starts to tap her toes. She hums a rhythm out loud. Her body casually sways with the music as her feet lead the way.

Shuffle hop step, shuffle hop step, dig, dig, and flap.

A few people watch her move with curiosity. She continues, unaware.

Hop shuffle toe, heel, heel, stomp.

"Gisela!" a voice calls.

Gisela doesn't even notice.

"Gisela!" the voice calls again.

Gisela continues to tap in her own little world. A hand touches her shoulder.

"Gisela."

Gisela hops and shudders, startled by the strange hand. She spins around to face ballet mistress Juliet.

"Ballet mistress."

"Your name is Gisela isn't it? You're Tatiana's daughter."

"Yes, but my name is Zel."

"I could have sworn it said Gisela on the roster. In fact, I remember when your mother became pregnant with you and talked about naming you after the famous ballet,Giselle," Juliet says.

"It says Gisela, but my name's Zel."

"Does your mother call you that?"

No.

"She's working on it," Gisela lies.

"Headed to class I presume," Juliet says.

Gisela's eyes shift as she thinks.

Not yours.

"Uh, huh."

"Lovely, let's walk together then," Juliet suggests.

Oh, wouldn't that be dandy…not!

"Sounds great." Gisela tries to fake a smile but it quickly turns to a frown as they start to walk out of the subway station side by side.

* * * * * * * * * * * * * * * * *

The ballet class is full. Everyone stands at the barre and walks through a tendu sequence. Meaghan starts in first position. She looks down at her feet, they curve in slightly. She sucks in, stands taller and turns her feet out further so they reach a full 180-degree line.

The music begins. Meaghan presents her arms and shines with utter joy and excitement, as if on stage performing for an audience of thousands.

Phillipe stands against the mirror and watches her. He leans into Juliet.

"The new girl is fantastic. So full of life."

"She's forcing her turnout," Juliet whispers back.

"At least she's forcing it herself. No one needing to correct her. She's trying."

Juliet groans.

"She glows, Juliet. When was the last time you saw that?" Phillipe asks.

"Tatiana," she replies.

"Exactly."

They both look to Gisela who tendus to the back and closes to a clean fifth.

"It's natural for her. She just has to want it," Juliet comments.

"But does she?" Phillipe says.

Meaghan lifts to a battement and lowers to a passé then relevés, lifts her arms to high fifth and holds the position.

Knee out.

She ever so slightly pushes her knee further out to the side. She lifts her chin, confidently.

* * * * * * * * * * * * * * * * * *

Meaghan wobbles around her dorm room, legs turned out. She clutches her hips.

"So much pain."

One of her roommates, Priscilla, offers a heating blanket.

"You can use it if you want. Helps minimize the muscle swelling," she says.

"I'll be okay, thanks. Just working on my turnout. My hips don't give as easy as some," Meaghan says.

Meaghan hobbles over to a chair against the wall and sits down. A drop of water hits her head. She looks up but doesn't see anything. She shakes her head. A drop of water hits her head again.

"What is that?"

"What's what?" Priscilla asks.

Meaghan looks up. A water drop hits her face, "That."

Priscilla puts her hand out. A couple drops fall on it. She looks down at the floor and there's a small puddle forming.

"That's not good."

All of a sudden, there's a clanging of metal. The girls both look up. The pipe bursts and water pours down on them. Both girls scream but are frozen in their positions. The water slows down to a mere dripping. Meaghan looks at Priscilla.

"I told you I felt something."

They both look at each other and start to laugh.

"Sorry, this is my rotten luck," Meaghan says.

Priscilla looks over at her soaked bunk bed.

"I've always wanted a water bed," she jokes.

The door swings open and one of the chaperones, Miss Nancy, stares at the room, a horrified look on her face.

"What in God's name has been going on in here?"

"Well…" Meaghan starts.

* * * * * * * * * * * * * * * * * *

Paige, Lori and Gisela sit on the floor playing Angry Birds on Paige's iPad.
"Level 10?" Gisela asks.
"The boomerang bird." Lori says.
"Man, I suck at video games."
The girls giggle.
On the lower bunk, Kelsi paints her toenails a fiery red color, and looks over Paige's shoulder at the game.
There's a knock at the door.
"Come in," Gisela yells.
Meaghan stands in the doorway with a duffle bag thrown over her shoulder and a rolling suitcase at her side. Water still drips from her messy red hair. She smiles, uncomfortably.
"Hi guys."

* * * * * * * * * * * * * * * * * *

A cot is in the center of the room leaving the girls very little space in the room to move around.
"This is ridiculous. This room is meant for four, not five. And it was hardly manageable with four, already. I doubt the fire department would approve of this," Paige complains.
"I'm really sorry," Meaghan says.
"It's not your fault," Lori says and pats her back. "We'll make it work for the meantime."
"Yeah, it's not like they'll keep you on this cot forever," Gisela adds.
"I'll take the cot if you don't like it," Kelsi offers. "It'll give me more room underneath for my stuff."
"No!" Paige, Gisela and Lori all say at the same time.
They look up at Kelsi's bunk. Clothes hang over the side; she has dirty towels and shoes all over the floor. Kelsi frowns.
"Well, I don't like this one bit. I say we complain to the management," Paige says.
"Do whatever you want," Lori laughs.
"Can we use your bed to finish our game?" Gisela asks Meaghan. "We were kinda in the middle of a level when you came in."
"Yeah, sure, go ahead," Meaghan says. She looks around the room, unsure what to do. She tries to walk to one of the lower bunks but her hip locks in place.
Day one. Body cannot move. So sore. This isn't good.

CHAPTER 10: ANGRY BIRDS

Gisela taps around the cramped room, practicing a rift combination. Kelsi and Paige sit on the roll-away cot and play cards. Lori quietly reads a book on her bed. Meaghan is stripped down to her bra and panties. She applies tiger balm to her entire body. The odor begins to move through the room.

"Eeewww, what is that rancid smell?" Paige asks. She holds her nose with one hand and plays the game with the other.

"The delightfully disgusting smell of tiger balm to make you want to throw up," Lori says.

Paige spins her head to look at Lori.

Did she just say what I think she said?

"Yeah, sorry again. I'm just so sore. My muscles are torn and this helps relax them so they don't stiffen up more," Meaghan says.

Paige continues to look at Lori. She looks her up and down.

Why would she say that? "Make you want to throw up."

"Breathe through your mouth and you won't notice," Gisela says while she taps around Meaghan who continues to apply more tiger balm.

A huge whiff of tiger balm floats over to the girls playing cards on the bed.

"I can't take this anymore!" Paige yells.

She throws down her iPad. Everyone stops what they're doing and stares at her.

"Are you okay?" Kelsi asks.

"No, I'm not okay. I'm not okay with having five people in this tiny little closet of a room. I'm not okay with your stuff everywhere, Kelsi," Paige rants. "I'm not okay with that horrible smell. I'm not..."

"Okay, with your hogging the bathroom," Lori interrupts. "or your constant tapping, Zel."

"Or your..." Gisela searches for something. "You're always being right." She glares at Lori.

Meaghan watches the chaos of the girls yelling at one another.

What is going on here? I think I was put in the crazies' room.

The girls continue to bicker.

"But, you..."

"No, I didn't."

"You stink."

"I can't believe..."

"It's your fault..."

"But you started it!"

"Girls, girls, girls!" Miss Nancy says as the door swings open. "What is going on in here?"

There's a moment of silence, then they all start to talk at once.

"She started it!"

"I did not."

"Did too!"

"Get her out!"

"And then she said…"

"I hate that smell."

"Quiet!" Miss Nancy screams.

The girls all fall silent and drop their flailing arms.

"I don't know what's going on in here and honestly, I don't care. One way or another, you all have to work this out, because you're stuck together for eight weeks. So like it or not, this is where you're living. These are your roommates. Try to get along."

She looks each girl straight in the eyes.

"And I'd better not hear another peep tonight from this room or you'll all be reprimanded. Got it?"

She makes eye contact with each girl again. Kelsi and Meaghan nod, scared. Paige bites her lip. Lori and Gisela say "yes" at the same time.

"Now, I suggest you get some sleep, because Mr. Morin will be casting for the showcase performance tomorrow. If you want a good part in the end of summer show, you'd best be at your finest."

Meaghan's eyes widen like a deer caught in the headlights. Gisela's eyes wander. She searches for an answer.

"Goodnight," Miss Nancy closes the door.

The girls relax and slowly retreat to their bunks. All are lost in thought. Paige sits up in her bed. "And I better not hear another peep or you'll be reprimanded," she mocks.

The girls giggle.

"Sorry for going off on you, Meaghan. And Kelsi."

"It's alright," Kelsi says, "I do need to pick up my stuff more. I'm so used to being messy at home."

As the girls continue to chat, Gisela lies in bed and stares at the ceiling. *What am I going to do? I have to choose. Tap or ballet.*

CHAPTER 11: SHOWCASE AUDITIONS

Lori, Paige, and Kelsi all stand in front of the mirror in the bathroom and primp themselves.

Think like your sisters. Perfection on the wood floor. Lori thinks.

Paige turns and looks at her profile.

Light as a feather, thinner than paper. Think thin thoughts, she tells herself.

Kelsi applies shiny lip gloss to an otherwise unmade -up face.

Give it your all. Dance like there's no tomorrow. She says to herself over and over again.

Meaghan opens a bottle of Tylenol and pours a couple into her hand. She dumps them in her mouth and swallows them down without any water.

Gisela grabs her cell phone and walks out into the hallway. She dials and puts it to her ear.

"Hi, this is Zel Palente, can you please just let Alan know that I won't be able to make it…at all this summer. But that I'd love to come back next summer."

She fights back a tear.

"Yes, that's all. Thanks."

She looks down at the phone then closes it.

Goodbye tap. Watch out ballet, here I come.

Determination fills her eyes and pushes away all her tears.

* * * * * * * * * * * * * * * * * *

The Russian woman goes through a combination for the audition.

"And a balancé, balancé, step battement, slide into an arabesque turn.

Finish and peek under."

She peeks under her raised arm then steps up on her toes and lifts to passé and closes back.

"Sissonne. Tombé pas de bourrée. Prep. Double pirouette."

She looks at all the girls who follow along and mark on their own.

"Repeat two times. Finish with five chaîné turns and two piqué turns followed by a chasse and the leap of your choice. After you've auditioned, you are welcome to return to the dorms. We are done for the day following this."

Phillipe and a few staff members including Juliet, sit on chairs against the mirror.

"Groups of three, please."

Gisela lines up with the first group. She takes the lead as the center point of the threesome. The Russian woman claps and the music begins. Gisela takes off with intensity.

Gisela dances her way through the combination the first time with determination and poise.

Juliet writes on her notepad. "Zel - fierce."

The second time through the combination she gives it even more power.

Take   that.

Gisela finishes with a stag jump where her back foot kicks her in the back of the head. Phillipe leans into Juliet.

"She's got so much punch you might even be worried about one like that."

"Except you remember her mother, don't you?" Juliet replies and smiles.

"Very true." Phillipe nods. "Very true."

The second group prepares. Meaghan is in the back. She takes in a deep breath.

Pain, pain go away, please come back no other day.

She bites her lip. The music begins. She takes another deep breath and then showcases a beautiful, gentle smile. She lifts her chin, confidently on her battement and pushes her turnout on the arabesque turn.

Twist hip!

She lifts her leg as she peeks under her arm holding an arabesque. Her toe wings up.

Ouch.

The Russian woman talks with Juliet, "New girl isn't too shabby."

"Terrible turnout. Sway back. No arches," Juliet replies.

"Yeah, but you can just feel her passion. It's exciting."

"Yes, but..."

"She's working harder than every other girl here," The Russian woman says defensively.

"Because she has to."

Meaghan finishes with a large pas de chat. She closes her landing fifth position as tight as she possibly can. She smiles and clutches her fist.

Yeah, I did it.

Meaghan jogs happily in an almost skip-like manner out of the room. She smiles at the staff along the mirror as she passes.

Paige prepares with her group and presents her arms as the music begins.

Out in the hallway, Meaghan clutches a hip and thigh. She cringes in pain.

Man that hurt.

She takes in a couple of deep breathes to calm herself and relax her muscles.

Come on Tylenol. Help me out here.

Meaghan reaches in her bag and pulls out a couple more Tylenol. She pops them in her mouth and swallows.

Back inside the room, Paige completes every step to perfection. She looks like a light, little fairy dancing about. Every movement is light and airy as if she was weightless and defied all gravity.

Juliet writes on her notepad, "Paige - perfect."

Paige finishes her jump, curtsies and leaves the room.

Meaghan is already gone when Paige walks out into the hallway.

"Good job," Priscilla says as she starts to down the hall.

"Thanks. You too," Paige says. She turns to head the opposite way. All of a sudden her vision blurs.

Whoa.

She blinks and it's black.

What's going on here? What's…?

She takes a step and falls into the wall. She hits the wall and shakes her head then untangles her legs and stands up.

What the heck?

She looks around, no one is in sight.

That was weird.

Back in the classroom, Lori begins the combination. She is unfocused.

Battement, step, balancé, balancé.

She looks to the left and realizes the other two girls are going the opposite way peeking under their arms in arabesque.

Shoot.

She slides into her arabesque three beats behind as the other two lift to passé.

Oh no. This is terrible.

Worry comes across her face and she dances with a scrunched forehead.

Lori preps for her double pirouette.

Piece of cake.

She spots her first turn nicely, then starts to lose balance on her second turn. Her supporting leg lowers from relevé and her working leg drops from passé.

Lori's eyes fill with tears as she does her chaîné and piqué turns.

"Nightmare." One of the staff members writes on her notepad as she elbows Juliet. Juliet quickly writes, "Corps" in response. They both nod.

Kelsi steps up with the next group. She closes her eyes for a moment.

You're on stage.

The music begins. She opens her eyes in a flash and there's an instant spark. She scrunches her nose then purses her lips and dances with a haughty attitude. She shines like a movie star on screen.

"She should be on Broadway," The Russian woman whispers to Phillipe.

"Her technique needs work, but I like her," Phillipe says. "I like her a lot."

The Russian woman writes "Lead" on her notepad. Juliet spots her note.

"Sure you want to deal with that?" Juliet asks.

"Phillipe has a vision," she replies. They both look at Phillipe. His eyes are full of life watching Kelsi jump higher than the other girls in her sissone.

"She does have something," Juliet says. "Question is can she handle the pressure."

Kelsi finishes with a bang. She chaînés into a grande jeté back leg bent and rolls to the floor out of it.

"Not quite ballet," The Russian woman says.

"It's okay to break the rules every now and then," Phillipe chuckles.

CHAPTER 12: CASTING

Meaghan wraps her legs and hips with plug-in heating pads. She lies on her cot in pain.

"Any better?" Lori asks.

Meaghan shakes her head, "My stomach hurts now."

"Want some Tums; I think I have a bottle?"

"That's alright. I just took a couple Tylenol. It should go away soon I bet."

Meaghan flashes a fake smile then turns her head into her pillow and groans.

A cell phone rings.

"Phone!" Paige yells.

"Not mine!" Kelsi calls from the bathroom.

"It's me," Lori says as she digs through a small bag to find the phone.

"Hello," she says into the phone.

Mrs. Clark walks the streets of New York City and talks on her phone.

"Darling, how are you?"

"Mom?" Lori says.

Meaghan sits up in bed. Gisela and Paige quickly sit on her cot as well.

"Of course,it's me. Who else would it be? Oh darling, I miss you so."

"You do?" Lori raises her eyebrows.

Gisela, Meaghan and Paige look at her interested.

"Honey, I'm just a block away why don't we go out for lunch? I phoned earlier and they said you had a day off due to auditions yesterday. I can't wait to hear all about how it went."

Lori's face drops.

"Meet me outside in ten," Mrs. Clark says.

"Okay. Okay, mom," Lori says. The girls sit on the edge of Meaghan's cot anxiously waiting to hear the news.

Lori closes her phone and puts it back in her bag.

"So…" Meaghan says.

"It was my mom."

"Yeah, we got that much," Gisela says.

"She wants to have lunch," Lori says, uninterested.

"Ah, how sweet," Gisela says.

"I wish my mom could take me to lunch here," Meaghan comments.

I wish my mom called me. Paige thinks.

Lori searches around and grabs a light sweater.

"Why so down? You should be excited," Paige says.

Kelsi pops her head out of the bathroom. "Really, I'd love to have a lunch with my mom. Someone to vent to and shop with. You know- girl talk."

"She wants to know how the audition went," Lori says.

"Oh," They all say at once.

"She's gonna think I'm such a disappointment because my sisters are so good. What should I tell her?" Lori asks.

"Tell her you don't know what you'll be yet. That's the truth. They said it wouldn't be posted until 11," Paige says.

"Yeah, we can text you when we find out if you want," Gisela offers.

"Okay." Lori smiles. "Thanks girls." She wraps her arms around them in a group hug.

Lori puts on her sweater, grabs a purse and heads for the door.

"See ya later."

"Bye."

"Have fun."

"Eat some yummy food for us!"

They all wave. Lori leaves.

"Poor thing. Her mom's gonna let her have it," Meaghan says. "I know the type. My friend's mom is like that."

I wish my mom was. Paige thinks.

She sighs.

Kelsi comes out of the bathroom. "Five minutes till eleven girls….."

They all get excited. Gisela taps her feet against the bed. "Last one there is in the corps!" Kelsi says.

The girls all rush out of the room. Meaghan hobbles out trailing behind the rest.

* * * * * * * * * * * * * * * * * *

The hallway is crowded with girls staring at a piece of paper posted on the wall. Kelsi makes it to the wall first. She scans down the list and sees her name. She runs her finger across the page; it reads "Pas de trois."

"Woohoo, pas de trois!"

She hugs a random person walking down the hall in her excitement.

Paige and Gisela look at the paper at the same time. They turn to each other, mouths open in awe. "Pas de trois!" they squeal.

"Me, too!" Kelsi says. She runs into a huddle with Paige and Gisela.

"I'm so excited!" Paige says. "I've always wanted to do a pas de trois."

"Me, too." Gisela says.

"Me, three." Kelsi adds. "What is a pas de trois?"

"It's a trio," Gisela says.

"A trio? So all three of us…" Kelsi jumps up and down.

"You crack me up, Kels," Paige says.

Meaghan stumbles to the wall and manages to squeeze in between a couple other girls.

Priscilla stands at the wall beside her. "That means the only solo goes to…."

"Me?" Meaghan says as she looks at the paper. "I got the solo."

She turns and looks at the girls. They all smile widely.

"I got the solo!"

Kelsi rushes her with a hug.

"Oh, I'm so excited for you!"

"Careful Kels, she's breakable," Paige says.

All the girls give Meaghan hugs.

"You're so lucky," Paige says.

"You deserve it," Gisela tells her. "And it's taught by my mom's friend. You'll love her, she's amazing."

"I can't believe it," Meaghan says, "I'm gonna go check again and make sure it's not a mistake."

Paige grabs her arm. "It's not a mistake. You're the soloist. Congrats."

Meaghan smiles a grin so wide it overtakes her face. Her cheeks are rosy.

"Anyone see where Lori was placed?" Kelsi asks.

Paige nods, "Understudy."

"To who?" Meaghan asks.

"To you," Paige says.

"Me?" Meaghan says shocked. "But she's so much better than me. Her feet are naturally arched and her arms are perfect and she has turnout to die for and…"

"And you got the role," Gisela says.

She smiles, "She's in the corps, too."

"Who wants to text her?" Kelsi asks.

"Well, since you brought it up, I nominate you. Oh, and let's celebrate. Ice cream on me!" Paige pulls out a credit card and waves it in the air.

"Yeah!" Meaghan squeals.

* * * * * * * * * * * * * * * * * * *

The girls sit around and enjoy ice cream cones, except Paige who eats a humongous ice cream sundae covered in hot fudge, whipped cream and cherries. She gobbles down on it and rubs her stomach.

"Oh man, is this good."

"Nice call, Paige. Thanks," Meaghan says as she raises her cone.

"To all of us kicking butt at the audition," Kelsi says. They all raise their cones. Paige raises her spoon. "Here, here." She then resumes eating her sundae at a ferocious speed.

"Okay, I am officially stuffed like a Thanksgiving turkey," Gisela groans.

"My stomach hurts too, but good pain this time," Meaghan puffs out her cheeks in a pretend sick way as she leans back in her chair.

Paige continues to shovel the ice cream in. She has whipped cream on her nose and ice cream all over her mouth. She looks up for a second to take a breath.

"You got a little something..." Meaghan points to her nose.

Paige touches her nose and sees the whipped cream on her finger. "Excuse me," she says politely and stands. She walks toward the bathroom inside the ice cream shop.

"I've never seen her eat that much of anything," Kelsi comments.

"She must really like ice cream," Meaghan replies.

Gisela looks toward the bathroom suspiciously, "You know, I have to use the restroom too. Be back in a second."

Gisela heads into the bathroom. She looks around, no one in sight. She starts to look under the stalls for feet. The sound of barfing is heard.

Gisela spots Paige's pretty petite Mary Janes under the stall door.

"Paige."

Paige gags for a second then tries to compose herself.

"Paige, I know what you're doing."

"I just ate too much is all. I have stomachache. I told you I have a nervous stomach. I'm overexcited. It happens," Paige replies.

"You shouldn't be doing this to yourself. It's not healthy."

"I'm fine."

"No you're not."

"I'm fine!" Paige screams. "Just please leave."

Paige begins to cry, "Please leave."

Gisela walks out of the bathroom and past the girls' table, "Be right back. Gotta make a call."

She pulls out her cell phone and dials as she walks out of the ice cream shop.

"Mom?" Gisela says. "Yeah, everything's fine. It's great actually. I was cast in a pas de trois choreographed by Phillipe Morin himself…thanks…yeah, it will be great…hey mom, I have a friend here who's throwing up, she's been doing it a lot and…I tried…you will? You'll talk to her? Thanks. Yeah, her name is Paige…yeah, that's the one I told you about…thanks. Oh, who called?… the tap studio called? What'd they say?…an audition, I'd love to audition for a commercial!… Why did you tell them I couldn't?… But it's on the weekend. I could still…okay, mom; yeah, I will…love you, too. Bye."

Gisela looks around at the bustling city.

"Me, in a commercial. Tapping. I can do that."

She dials on her phone again.

"Hello? Hi, Alan? It's Zel…yeah, sorry, about the mix-up; I'd love to come Saturday. Where is it at again?"

Gisela concentrates hard.

"Okay, I'll be there. Wouldn't miss it for the world…thanks again."

She smiles.

321 Upton Street. 321 Upton Street. I better go write this down.

Gisela rushes inside and goes to the counter.

"Do you have a pen I can borrow?"

The man behind the counter passes her a pen. She grabs a napkin and writes down "321 Upton, Saturday @ 1:00 pm."

She hands back the pen. "Thanks."

She holds the napkin to her chest and takes in a deep breath.

Finally.

CHAPTER 13: BODY ISSUES

Gisela looks at MapQuest on her phone. "So, to get to Main, I'd need to take the subway and then from there I could hop on a bus to 2nd, and hail a cab from 2nd to Upton." She moves the map around. "Or,….nah, too complicated."

She sits down on her bed. "If I leave at 11:30 I should get there with plenty of time, I think."

She stares off, lost in thought.

"Secret boyfriend?" Kelsi asks.

"Noo. Ewwww" Gisela laughs. "I don't like boys and they don't like me."

"You kidding? You're gorgeous. Guys will fall all over you in high school. There were two guys drooling all over you just at the ice cream shop the other day."

"No, they weren't." Gisela says.

"Uh, yeah. They were. When you got up to go to the bathroom they were practically drooling like dogs waiting for steak as they watched you walk away. You look way older than thirteen." Gisela laughs, "You're silly. Besides, my mother would never allow me to have a boyfriend. She fell in love young and wound up pregnant with yours truly. Ruined her whole ballet career. She was a prima ballerina for the Company you know."

"No, way."

"Way. Everyone loved her. She was…stunning. And now everyone wants me to be just like her."

"Bet that's a lot of pressure."

"Not too bad, actually, I just don't want to be a ballerina. I want to tap, that's the problem."

"Rehearsal time." Meaghan pops her head in the door.

"Aren't you supposed to be rehearsing right now?" Kelsi asks.

"On break."

Meaghan grimaces.

"You alright?"

Meaghan shakes her head. "Stomach feels like it's eating itself." Meaghan goes to grab her bottle of Tylenol.

"Maybe you should lay off the Tylenol a bit," Kelsi suggests.

"But then, how will I deal with the pain in my hips?" Meaghan pops a couple more Tylenol.

Gisela and Kelsi watch her swallow the pain meds without water.

"How do you do that?" Kelsi asks. "Just watching you I am gagging."

"Easy. I live off these things."

Gisela and Kelsi grab their dance bags and head to the studio.

* * * * * * * * * * * * * * * * * *

Lori is at the back of the room following Paige.

"She's following Paige now, too?" Kelsi whispers to Gisela as they enter.

"She's understudying the whole cast." Gisela says, "Poor girl is exhausted."

Phillipe claps his hands, "Very good. Now that the others are here, we can review what we added yesterday."

Gisela and Kelsi slip on their ballet slippers and take their places on either side of Paige. Phillipe claps his hands and the pianist begins to play.

The three join hands and begin a complicated sequence of battement frappés and fondues. Lori mimics them in the back.

All three girls hold their upper bodies super stiff. They make themselves appear weightless. Gisela and Paige's footwork is perfectly in-sync. Kelsi falls behind and crosses feet with Paige causing her to stumble.

Phillipe claps his hands and the music stops.

"Is there a problem?" he stares at Kelsi.

She shakes her head. "Just got behind a count."

"More than one count. Let's try it again."

The girls scoot back and join hands. The pianist begins to play the same music. They dance the battement frappé sequence exactly the same. Kelsi misses a step. She stops and tries to catch up. Phillipe turns to Juliet, "I think I made a mistake in casting." Juliet raises an eyebrow, "You think?" she says sarcastically.

Phillipe claps his hands and the music stops. Kelsi bites her lip.

"What are we going to do here, Kelsi?" Phillipe asks.

"I'll practice more, I promise."

"You better. Performance is just a couple weeks away."

He looks back at Lori. "Just for fun, let's bring you in and see how you do." He motions to Lori.

Me.

She points at herself, unsure.

He nods, "Yes, please. Humor me."

Kelsi reluctantly steps aside. Lori takes her place and joins hands with Paige and Gisela. The music begins. The three perform the sequence beautifully. Every step is in-sync, every head movement perfectly placed. Kelsi watches, she nervously twitches.

Phillipe applauds. "Very nice. That," he looks at Kelsi and gestures to the trio, "is what it's supposed to look like."

He nods to Lori. She curtsies.

"Now, you three get out of here and onto costume fittings. Juliet has rehearsal."

Meaghan steps out into the middle of the room.

"Let's take it from the bourrée section."

Meaghan pops up to a sous sous. A fast, upbeat music begins. Meaghan beats her feet into the ground squeezing her thighs together then breaks into a series of fast entrechats. She lands in fifth. The music softens. She développés her right leg up into the air. Her leg extends a la seconde up to her ear. She holds the pose for a moment then elevés and lowers her leg right into a petite jeté combo as the music quickens again.

Juliet raises her hand to the pianist. The music stops.

"Very good. Let's just go through the petite jetés again. Be careful your foot doesn't sickle as you brush the floor."

Meaghan grimaces in pain.

"Are you alright?" Juliet asks.

Meaghan bends over and breathes.

"Fine. My stomach is just cramping really bad. It's been like this for days though."

She walks back into the center of the room.

"Now, where did you want to start again?" Meaghan asks.

She suddenly doubles over and grabs her stomach.

"We'll start by getting you to the doctor," Juliet says and guides her to the door.

* * * * * * * * * * * * * * * * * *

A short Asian man stands before Meaghan who sits on a small, uncomfortable examination table wearing a paper thin gown.

"Your body has pain to tell you that you're hurting yourself. Forcing your turn out by pushing areas to the limit and beyond is causing damage to your hips and knees. This is very serious for someone so young and can affect you for the rest of your life if you continue in this way. The best medicine for you right now is rest, and no more Tylenol. Your stomach can't handle any more of that. Got it?"

She nods her head.

"Just stop overworking your joints and the swelling will reduce so the healing can begin. For best results, I'd suggest staying away from strenuous activities for at least six weeks."

But that showcase is in three weeks. I'm a soloist. I'm the soloist.

She stares off in a daze.

"Meaghan. Meaghan," The doctor calls.

She shakes her head and he comes into focus.

"Any questions?"

"No, doctor. Thank you. No more Tylenol."

She hops off the examination table and walks out of the office.

* * * * * * * * * * * * * * * * * *

Kelsi, Paige and Gisela all pull on a stretchy, jersey material leotard dress. The seamstress begins to pull down on Kelsi's and write notes on her paper.

"Take out an inch here."

She measures with a ruler. "Another half inch here and let's see…" She looks at the ruler more closely, "Two inches here."

She looks up at Kelsi. "What did I tell you? Stay the same size. You've lost two inches since you've been here. Eyyye yay yay."

Paige looks at her, jealously. Kelsi shrugs.

"It's the healthy lunches. I eat biscuits and gravy for lunch back home."

Paige looks at herself in the mirror as the seamstress adjusts Gisela's costume. The material clings to her body, exposing every little ounce of muscle and meat. Paige looks at Gisela and Kelsi. Both look very thin in their costumes. She looks at herself in the mirror again. Although she too is very slender, she doesn't see it. In her eyes, the image she sees is like a trick mirror making large things look small and small things like gigantic.

No more lunch for me.

* * * * * * * * * * * * * * * * *

Meaghan lays in bed on her cot when the other girls come in, all except

Lori.

"Are you alright?" Gisela asks. "We just saw Lori in the hall and she said you were sent to the doctor."

"I'm fine."

The girls look concerned.

They'll think I'm weak.

"It was just a stomach bug doc said. He gave me some meds to take. Said don't worry about it."

I'm going to hell for lying.

"I'm not contagious I promise."

At least that much isn't a lie.

"Good. We want to make sure you're healthy for your big solo debut in a couple weeks," Kelsi says.

Meaghan smiles, "Night guys. I'm really tired."

She pulls the sheet over her head and looks down at her feet tied to the end of the bed.

Pull me through body, do your job.

CHAPTER 14: PRESSURE

Meaghan performs for Juliet. She extends her develop a la seconde and holds it. She elevés and her knee buckles. She falls to the ground and clutches her knee for a moment. Juliet rushes over to her. Lori watches from the back, worried.

"It's fine," Meaghan says. "Can I just have a second to wrap it?"

"Absolutely."

Meaghan hobbles over to the side and pulls a nude-colored bandage wrap out of her bag. She wraps her left knee tightly and secures the end of the wrap with a metal clasp.

She stands up and walks just fine on the knee. She resumes her place with the dance.

"Let's take it again from the same spot."

Meaghan extends her développé a la seconde and holds it. She elevés, her knee buckles again. She falls hard over the knee. A crack is heard.

"It's fine," Meaghan cries out.

Juliet motions her finger at Lori to come here. Lori jogs to the center of the room.

"Would you, please?" Juliet asks.

Lori nods. Meaghan scoots herself to the side. The music begins and Lori dances. Tears fall down Meaghan's cheeks as Lori dances perfectly.

Keep this up and I'm going to let everyone down again.

Kelsi steps into the doorway and watches Lori dance as well. She leans and sighs, as Lori brings the movements to life with sophistication beyond her years.

I'll see if she can help me. Nights, weekends, whatever it takes.

* * * * * * * * * * * * * * * * * *

Paige has another fitting. She looks at herself in the mirror and feels fat.
Look at how it clings against my butt.
She spins and looks at her costume from all angles.
Ugh, and those thunder thighs. This makes them even worse.
She sneers in the mirror, erasing her beautiful image.
No more carbs, no fruit…too many carbs and grams of sugar. No processed meat, no dairy.
She smoothes down the front of her costume. Her hands focus on the abdominal section.
Terrible. 600 crunches a day.
She looks in the mirror once more and sighs.

* * * * * * * * * * * * * * * * * *

Gisela packs her tap shoes in a bag and looks over a handwritten set of directions. She looks in the mirror.
I need Kelsi.

* * * * * * * * * * * * * * * * * *

Gisela sits on top of the toilet seat in the bathroom. Kelsi stands in front of her and applies sparkly eye shadow from the biggest make up bag Zel has ever seen.
"There, perfect. A subtle glow to simply highlight your natural beauty."
Gisela turns around and looks in the mirror, she's stunning. Natural and beautiful, just like Kelsi said. She stares at herself in amazement.
"Wow. I never knew I could look like this."
"Your date will love it," she jokes.
I really miss doing make-up and hair and wearing my costumes. And dancing to music with words!
"Earth to Kels," Zel smiles as she looks at the time on her cell phone.
"I have to run."
"Good luck! Break a leg," Kelsi calls as Gisela heads out the door.
"Now my turn for a favor," she says.
Lori dances alone in a dark studio. Kelsi opens the door bringing in some light. Lori immediately stops.
"Thought I'd find you here."
"Yeah, just getting an extra workout in," Lori says shyly.
Kelsi shifts her feet nervously.

"You did really well in my spot the other day," she says. "Phillipe wishes he had picked you. I know he does."

"No. He saw something special in you. We all do. You just have to practice more," Lori says.

"Besides, I messed up my audition. I deserve to be an understudy."

"That's not true."

Lori shrugs.

"I know it's asking a lot, but do you think, I mean, would you mind helping me?"

Lori smiles.

"I'm just afraid Phillipe is going to kick me out otherwise. I mean if you don't want to don't..."

"I'd love to," Lori interrupts.

Kelsi hugs her, "Thank you so much."

* * * * * * * * * * * * * * * * * *

Gisela sits on the dirty lobby floor of an old building. She double-knots her tap shoes, then opens her legs out into a butterfly position and bounces her thighs. She looks around at everyone else as she stretches.

Look at all these people. What am I doing here?

Most of the other dancers are older. A short, chunky woman emerges from a door down the hall. She walks into the lobby. Everyone turns their attention to her.

"Hi everyone, thanks for coming out on a Saturday."

Several dancers smile at her, clinging to her every word.

"What we're going to do is take you back and teach you a combination. Then you'll come back here and we'll call you back one at a time to audition on camera. Any questions?"

A twenty-something woman raises her hand.

"Yes?" the casting director points to her.

"What is the commercial for?"

"Raisin Bran," the casting director replies. "First run national SAG scale."

"Cool, thanks," the woman says.

"Any other questions?"

No hands are raised.

"Alright, come on back then."

The dancers all stand and follow her into an industrial-space type room with high, open rafter ceilings and concrete walls.

Much to Gisela's surprise Alan stands at the front of the room.

Alan?

She stops and stares at him.

"Hurry and spread on out," Alan says. He looks around at the dancers and spots Gisela. She stares at him.

What?

He smiles and winks at her, then turns his back to the rest of the group.

"We have a lot to learn and very little time so make sure you can see me."

Gisela joins the rest of the group but winds up in the back of the pack where it's difficult to see.

"This is a fun, little combo, filled with lots of rhythm changes so pay close attention."

Alan begins a complicated sequence of rifts and shuffles. All the dancers' eyes are glued on his feet. Alan drags his right toe into his ankle and spins.

Gisela struggles to see Alan and keep up. She relies on the people in front of her and just catches bits and pieces of a rift combination. Gisela frowns and scrunches her forehead in frustration.

"Okay, let's try it with the music," Alan says.

Music already? But I don't even know what we're doing!

Gisela looks around at all the dancers, ready to burst out in tears.

Why did I even come? I'm not ready for this.

Gisela starts to walk away.

The music begins.

That sounds familiar.

She turns and watches the dancers start the routine.

Wait. I know that!

Suddenly it hits her; it's a combination from class.

I know that routine. I can do this!

Gisela jumps back onto the dance floor and joins in for the last few eight counts.

The music stops.

"Very good everyone," Alan says.

The dancers all clap politely. Gisela smiles and breathes a sigh of relief.

"Now, Raisin Bran wants this real lively and fresh, so we're gonna spice things up a bit, and do the routine double-time."

Several dancers moan. A guy near Gisela shakes his head, "There's no way." Gisela smirks.

Yes there is.

"I've only ever known one dancer who could do it on the first try. And honestly I don't know if anyone can do it better than her. So because of that I'll cut you a break. We'll practice it two times." He holds up two fingers.

"That's it!" the guy beside Gisela exclaims, astonished.

The dancers shake out their legs and arms, and roll back their shoulders to relax and ready themselves. Gisela stands with her arms folded across her chest and a big smile on her face.

I've got this.

The music starts at double-time. The dancers take a deep breath awaiting the count.

"A five, six, seven, eight," Alan says as she claps out the beats.

All the dancers, Gisela included, break into the routine. Most focus hard, a few tap confidently, but miss a dig or toe here and there. Gisela shines as she taps, full of utter joy.

* * * * * * * * * * * * * * * * * *

Kelsi stands with her arms outward, in a dark room. Lori lifts her elbows.

"Remember, elbows elevated like you're setting a tray of tea on them," Lori says.

"A tray of tea?"

"That's what living in England so long does to ya I guess? I love my tea just as much as any 'ol Brit."

"You miss it, don't you?"

Lori nods. "But it's good. I need a change for a while. Makes you stronger."

They share a moment of silence, lost in thought.

"Let's go through the pirouette section again."

Kelsi preps for a turn sequence.

* * * * * * * * * * * * * * * * * *

A few dancers remain in the lobby. Gisela sits on the ground hugging her knees into her chest and relaxing. A couple of the others continue to practice the routine. Gisela watches them.

Missed the dig heel on six.

Oh, there's no step there.

Man, your rhythm is way off.

"Zel Palente!" the casting director calls.

"Here." Gisela jumps up.

"You're up, dear."

Gisela follows her back into another room where there's a video camera set up.

"Stand on the 'X'," the casting director says.

Gisela looks for an 'X.' She spots two pieces of tape on the ground crossed in an 'X' pattern. She stands on the 'X.'

The casting director turns the video camera on and presses "record."

"Slate your name and age, please."

"Zel Palente. 13."

"I'll play the music and you just do your thing."

The casting director presses a button on a small stereo. The music plays.

Gisela taps aggressively, full of energy and personality. She giggles as she dances. She hits every beat perfectly. She finishes and is overwhelmed with emotion.

This is what I was meant to do.

"Why were you laughing?"

"I don't know. It just felt good to tap. It made me happy!"

The casting director smiles.

"Well, thank you for coming in. Callbacks will be later this afternoon. We'll call you if you're selected."

* * * * * * * * * * * * * * * * * *

Paige sits on the cafeteria with Priscilla, Meaghan and a couple other girls. They all eat, except Paige who stares at the plate of food in front of her. She licks her lips.

"Aren't you going to eat, Paige? The cottage cheese and peaches are extra yummy today."

Paige gulps hard, "I forgot I already ate. I'm full."

She looks at her plate again.

"Want some more?"

She pushes the plate in front of Priscilla, "I gotta run."

She rushes out of the cafeteria.

* * * * * * * * * * * * * * * * * *

Gisela sits on the bus when her cell phone rings.

"Zel?" the casting director on the other end of the line says.

"Yes?"

"We need you to come in for a callback. Be here in an hour."

"An hour? Okay. Thanks!"

Gisela closes her phone and squeals. The people around her look at her strangely.

"Now, I gotta get off this bus," she says as she stands up and makes her way to the front.

I got a callback. I got a callback!

CHAPTER 15: REHEARSAL

"Anyone hear how Zel's audition went Saturday? I forgot to ask her," Kelsi says as she pulls leg warmers on over her ballet slippers.

"I didn't even know she had an audition," Meaghan says.

"Yeah, who with? Dish," Lori says.

"I don't know. She asked me to do her make-up."

"Where is Zel by the way? And Paige at that?" Meaghan asks.

"Mr. Morin asked them to meet in his office before class."

"Are they in trouble?" Lori asks.

Meaghan shrugs her shoulders.

* * * * * * * * * * * * * * * * * * *

Paige and Gisela sit in large-cushioned chairs before a sizable polished wood desk. Mr. Morin sits behind the desk.

"You're not in trouble. In fact it's quite the opposite."

Paige relaxes.

"In order to market the upcoming showcase we have to put together some flyers and posters and such to get people interested and increase awareness. Each year we choose a few extraordinary students who also happen to have a certain look. This year the staff and I have chosen you."

"Me?" Gisela says.

"Me?" Paige says right after her.

"Both of you. We'd like you to be the faces of the showcase."

"Mr. Morin this is such an honor. Thank you so much, Gisela gushes.

"I don't know what to say," Paige mumbles. "I'm, I'm…"

"Speechless?" Phillipe fills in. "Just say yes."

Paige smiles. "Yes!"

"Good. Go and get your shoes then. The photographer's waiting in studio C."

"We're shooting now?" Gisela asks.

"Uh huh. Have to get it done quickly to get to the press."

"I have to go to the bathroom first," Paige says.

"Okay. Just ..." Phillipe starts.

"No, she doesn't," Gisela interrupts.

"Yes, I do," Paige glares at Gisela.

"Fine. I'm coming too," Gisela says.

Phillipe shakes his head.

"Go to the bathroom, don't, I don't care. Just get to studio C pronto."

The girls leave the room.

Paige heads toward the bathroom.

"You don't have to do that, Paige. It's bad for you."

"I have to pee," Paige says. She scowls and enters the bathroom.

Gisela sighs then heads down the hallway.

* * * * * * * * * * * * * * * * * *

Paige and Gisela pose for the photographer against a shiny metallic backdrop, filled with bright yellow circles and rust-colored streaks. Paige wears an orange leotard with attached tutu. Gisela dons a red bodysuit with a lifted collar. They hold odd, but elegant poses which look almost like something out of a fashion magazine.

"Now you lift your leg up," The photographer points at Paige.

She développés her leg sideways.

"And lift up on your toes," he says.

Paige elevés.

"Perfect."

The photographer snaps a couple shots.

Paige blinks. She blinks again.

"Try to keep your eyes open," the photographer says.

"I...I..."

Paige blinks quickly.

"I'm feeling a bit dizzy."

Gisela spins around and looks at her, "Paige?"

"Girls we really need to get on with this," the photographer says.

Paige's eyes flutter and roll into the back of her head.

"Paige!"

Paige falls over and hits the ground. Gisela drops to her knees beside her.

She checks her pulse.

"Call an ambulance!" she screams.

The photographer scurries out of the room.

Paige starts to move.

"Paige? Paige, can you hear me?" Gisela asks.

She opens her eyes and sits up quickly. She scrunches her nose as she tries to find her center of balance.

Gisela holds her back.

"Why are you holding me?" Paige asks.

Gisela can't help but smile.

"You're okay."

"What are you talking about?"

"You just fainted. We were taking pictures and you felt dizzy and the next thing I know you're on the ground," Gisela explains.

Paige's eyes widen.

"Don't tell anyone about this. They might think something's wrong. They might take me out of the performance."

"This is serious. You need help."

"You don't understand."

"Who could understand better? I'm here just like you," Gisela's eyes plead to make Paige trust her.

Let me help you.

Phillipe rushes into the room. "Ahhh, thank God you're alright."

He walks back and forth quickly.

"The ambulance is outside. Paramedics will be up any second to get you."

"That's not necessary. Like you said, I'm fine," Paige says.

Phillipe shakes his head. "We have to have you looked at. Otherwise…"

"Otherwise what?" Gisela asks.

"Legal stuff," Phillipe responds. "Zel, why don't you go back to the dorms now."

"But I want to go with her."

"It would really be best for you to return to your room," he says.

"But I saw it. I was a witness," she continues.

"Zel." He stares at her firmly.

"Fine."

She faces Paige, blocking Phillipe's view. "Call me if you need anything," she mouths.

"Thanks," Paige mouths back.

Gisela retreats down the hall, looking back as the paramedics arrive and begin poking at Paige.

* * * * * * * * * * * * * * * * * * *

Paige lies in a hospital bed with a disposable gown on.

"How long have you had this problem?" the doctor asks.

"What problem?" Paige says.

"The eating disorder. The bulimia."

"I don't do that, Paige retorts.

"I know you do. Your throat, the decay on the back of your teeth, the yellowing of your skin in certain places…all tell tale signs," the doctor says.

Paige grimaces.

"So, how long has it been?"

Paige lowers her head.

"I'm only trying to help you. How many times have you done it?"

Paige shrugs. "I don't know."

"Every day, twice a day, only after big meals?" The doctor fishes for an answer.

"It varies."

"Depending on what?"

"The mirror," Paige replies.

"The mirror? You mean how you think you look in the mirror?"

Paige nods. "And other things."

"Like what?"

"I'm really late for rehearsal and I can't be missing at a time like this, can I go now?" she asks.

"Since we don't have parental consent we technically can't keep you here."

"Good." Paige starts to sit up.

"But…let me strongly suggest that you lay off the exercise for awhile and see a nutritionist who can help you on the road to recovery and get you healthy again."

"Thanks," Paige says, sarcastically. "I'll do that."

She sits up completely and holds the blanket over her body.

"Do you mind?"

The doctor leaves the room.

* * * * * * * * * * * * * * * * * * *

Miss Nancy sits in the waiting room. Paige comes out fully dressed. "What'd they say?" she asks.

"I was just tired. Said I should get some iron tablets. Can we stop by the pharmacy on the way back?"

"Of course," Miss Nancy says.

They head out of the hospital.

Paige looks back, the doctor stands in the hallway with her chart and watches her walk off, worried.

I'm fine...I think.

CHAPTER 16: RESCUED BY FRIENDSHIP

Kelsi continues to practice with Lori in empty studios at night. Lori applauds her. Kelsi curtsies and the girls both break into a giggle fest. "Magnificent. I can read the headlines now…from push up bra to pointe shoes, a ballerina is born," Lori says.

Kelsi shoves her playfully, "Shut up. The sheet said pink tights and black attire. It was black."

"And tacky."

"Hey, low blow."

"You know I'm kidding," Lori says.

"I know. One more time?"

"Go for it."

Lori presses a button on a small stereo and the music plays. Kelsi begins the routine and dances like a star.

* * * * * * * * * * * * * * * * * *

In class, Kelsi performs with Paige and Gisela. The three look excellent together. Kelsi keeps up with the two and doesn't miss a step.

"Nice work, Kelsi." Phillipe says as he watches them.

Kelsi smiles.

Finally!

* * * * * * * * * * * * * * * * * *

Walking out of class, Paige gives Kelsi a high-five.

"Good stuff out there," she says. Kelsi hits Paige's hand really hard and throws her off balance. Paige feels dizzy for a moment but tries to hide it. She leans against a wall. The other girls continue back to the dorms.

"You comin'?" Kelsi asks.

"Be there in a minute. Just taking a breather," Paige lies.

Her vision is scattered and blurry. She takes in a deep breath of air.

Gisela exits the classroom, cell phone to her ear.

"Oh my God, I got it! I got it!" she says.

She doesn't even see Paige.

"Got what?" Paige asks.

Gisela continues down the hall on her phone, excitedly talking.

"It shoots on Saturday? Perfect…..And I need parental consent?"

Yikes. Mom will never agree.

"Would a chaperone work? I'm at ballet school."

Gisela waits with baited breath.

Please say yes. Please say yes.

"Really? That's great! Thank you so much."

Gisela closes her phone and begins to waltz down the hallway by herself, happily lost in her pure excitement.

Paige finally regains her vision completely. She remains leaning against the wall.

Wonder if I should eat something? Food does sound good.

* * * * * * * * * * * * * * * * *

Meaghan dances in front of Juliet. Lori copies in the back of the room. Meaghan développés her leg a la seconde and holds it a couple counts. She elevés then releases it in a swift, but controlled manner. Her upper body is perfectly lifted and she even smiles as she dances.

"Excellent," Juliet says.

"Thank you," Meaghan says.

"How'd you like a sneak peek at your costume?"

Meaghan nods her head, excitedly.

"You want to come too?" Juliet asks Lori.

"Yes, ma'am, I'd very much like that," Lori replies.

* * * * * * * * * * * * * * * * *

A classic white tutu and leotard hang up in the sewing room. Meaghan's jaw drops. "That's it?"

Juliet nods.

"It's…it's…"

"Incredible," Lori says.

"So you like it then?" Juliet asks.

Meaghan nods. "Can I touch it?"

"Carefully."

Meaghan approaches the hung-up tutu and leotard. The rhinestones on it sparkle in the light. Meaghan smiles gently.

Just like Angelina Ballerina.

She brushes her fingers across the beading.

Too beautiful for words.

Lori stands in the back and stares at the dress, eyes full of dreams.

Like Swan Lake.

"Want to try it on?" Juliet asks.

"Really?" Meaghan says.

"Uh, huh."

Meaghan nods her head crazily.

"I'll take that as a yes.

Meaghan jumps up and claps, excited.

Juliet takes the hangers off the hooks. She slowly removes the delicate beaded straps and holds the silk bodice.

"Step in," Juliet says. She holds the leotard open. Meaghan ever so slowly steps into the leotard. Her face glows as she looks at the costume. Juliet pulls the straps up and flattens the tutu. She steps and looks at Meaghan.

Meaghan is radiant. Despite her messy rehearsal hair, black leotard poking out under the white costume and mismatched tights, she is a dream.

I feel so pretty.

"How do I look?" she asks.

Lori stares at her and her eyes glaze over lost in thought.

That should be me. I want to wear the classic white tutu. Every girl dreams of being her and I should be. Everyone back home will be so disappointed. I'm a failure. I'm nothing like my sisters. They expected me to get the solo. They thought I'd be the star. Now, I'm nothing. I'm scenery.

"You look amazing." Juliet says. "And Lori, you will have your turn one day soon."

She looks incredible.

"Thanks," Meaghan says.

I feel like a princess. I actually feel like Angelina Ballerina for the first time in my life. I'm a real ballerina now.

* * * * * * * * * * * * * * * * * *

Lori talks on her cell phone outside the dorm room. She paces the hall.

"You always say that, mom."

Lori stops and strikes a pose with her hip out. She mocks her mother, "There are a thousand girls who would kill to dance any part onstage with the New York Company Ballet."

Lori groans.

"I'm just...I'm so frustrated. That should have been me but I screwed up."

A single tear streams down her cheek.

I've let everyone down.

Juliet sees Lori and thinks about going over to speak to her. Disappointment is a rough part of the dance world and no one is going to hold these girls hands. She decides to watch Lori closely for the next few days and make sure she is not too upset. These girls need to toughen in order to survive at this business, but crushing a dancer's spirit is NOT part of the summer curriculum.

CHAPTER 17: NO PAIN, NO GAIN

"Dress rehearsal day! And a showcase tonight! Get up girls. Rise and shine!" Kelsi yells. She bounces on Lori's bed, then Meaghan's cot, and Paige's bed. She tosses a sock up at Gisela on the top bunk. Meaghan sits up quickly. The rest open their eyes then roll back over in bed.

Kelsi looks around and smiles.

"Bacon and eggs!" she calls.

All four girls sit up tall.

"What? Where?" Paige asks.

"I love bacon!" Gisela says.

"Any pancakes?" Lori asks.

"Yep. And syrup," Kelsi says.

They all look around. Kelsi stares at them and smiles.

"Where's it at?" Paige asks.

"I don't know. Just thought that might get all you sleepyheads up."

They all moan and relax back in their beds.

"It's the big day! Aren't you guys excited? I can hardly stand still."

"Yeah, we noticed," Gisela says in an annoyed tone.

She pulls the covers back over her head.

* * * * * * * * * * * * * * * * *

The stage is lit and people scurry around trying to get the sets ready. The girls all sit in the audience and lean back in the chairs taking it all in.

"We all get to be ballerinas today," Meaghan says. "I've always wanted this, but wasn't sure it would come true."

"I thought I would be a doctor when I was little," Paige says. "I like

103

medicine and taking care of people."

Gisela looks over at her, "Really? What would your specialty be? Eating disorders?"

"Why would she want to deal with that? Boring," Kelsi says. "If I were a doctor I'd want to be in the ER and get all the cool, exciting stuff like the people coming in with gunshot wounds and pulling the bullets out and stuff."

The girls all turn and look at her strangely.

"You're a freak," Paige says.

Kelsi shrugs, "I know."

They all giggle.

"What about you, Lor?" Meaghan asks. "What did you want to be?"

Lori stares off blankly.

"I don't know. I never really had a choice. It was always ballet. I guess I just assumed that's what I should do because that's all I know. I've never been allowed to do much else."

Gisela frowns. "I know what you mean."

Phillipe stands on stage and looks out into the audience. "Time to get dressed."

The girls jump up and rush backstage.

* * * * * * * * * * * * * * * * * *

Lori poses with a large group of dancers. The music begins and they dance a simple, but unified routine.

"Watch your spacing." Phillipe points to a couple dancers. The girls move over and continue the routine.

Lori dances her best and stands out amongst the crowd. It's obvious she is better than the corps position she has been assigned. While her technique is perfect, her face is emotionless.

There are a thousand girls who would kill to have any role onstage with the New York Company Ballet. And I have it. I have what they want. Smile. Be happy.

She continues the routine and finishes, but a smile never graces her lovely face.

Kelsi, Paige and Gisela quickly run on their toes to the center of the stage. Lori poses in the back with the corps and watches.

"Downstage more Paige," Phillipe says. Paige takes a step forward. The three join hands and the music begins. All three look beautiful in their skin-tight costumes and their timing is impeccable. Paige looks very thin in comparison to her comrades. Almost breakable.

The pas de trois finishs. The staff in the audience claps. The girls run off stage along with the corps.

"Remember, corps, stay in the wings for the next segment!" Phillipe yells.

Meaghan's white ballet slippers slowly step out on stage, each step a deliberate action made with complete control. A spotlight centers over her. Meaghan poses, her wrists crossed out in front of her, right foot turned out pointing effacé.

The dancers all watch from the wings.

The music starts. Those watching in the wings smile as Meaghan leaps to her piqué and presents her arms to the audience with a delicate but commanding quality, which makes her look like a natural born star.

Ah ha!

Meaghan continues to dance with graceful power. She reaches the développé section. She extends her leg, raises her chin and elevés. She holds the pose for three beats then releases.

So, this is what this feels like.

Her leg swings around and continues in a glissade sequence. She finishes with a fouette turn combination where she changes her spot and rotates to all four directions. She finishes croisé back and flips her wrists with flair.

My mom is going to be so proud.

Everyone claps.

The rest of the dancers make their way on stage in rows doing synchronized chaîné turns. Everyone joins together and does a changement combination followed by a sous sous and pose. The music ends and new, cheerful music starts to play.

Meaghan curtsies and steps aside from her place in the front. Paige, Kelsi and Gisela curtsy and then step aside and point to the corps, who then curtsies as well.

Finally, everyone joins hands and bows together.

The curtain closes and the music ends.

"Alright, good run through. Open it up!" Phillipe yells.

The curtains reopen. All the dancers stand on stage talking.

"Everyone is done for the morning. Go back to the dorms and rest. We have a big show this evening."

The dancers all start to slowly make their way off stage. Phillipe approaches Meaghan.

"I'd like to run your solo one more time if you don't mind. The lighting was a bit off and I want to get it just right with the crew," Phillipe says.

"Sure, Mr. Morin."

* * * * * * * * * * * * * * * * * *

The theater is empty besides Meaghan on stage, Phillipe walking from the stage to the audience and the lighting crew in the back.

"Alright, let's take it from the beginning."

Meaghan crosses her wrists and places her foot behind her. The music begins.

Phillipe stands with the lighting technique in the sound booth at the back of the theater.

"Now, bring in the front dimmers."

The front lights begin to dim.

"White spot follow on her."

A white spotlight follows Meaghan as she dances.

"Now, add in some twinkles."

A set of twinkle lights spins around the stage.

Meaghan continues to dance, giving it her all.

"No, those are not the right ones." Phillipe continues. "Do you have a chart or something I can look at please?"

"Yeah," the tech says, "right here." He hands him a laminated lighting card with patterns on it. Phillipe studies the card.

Meaghan continues to dance even though no one is paying attention. She doesn't notice. She focuses hard on the steps at hand.

"Do you think number ten would work?" Phillipe asks the tech.

Meaghan extends her leg out and elevés. All of a sudden her knee gives out.

"Oh, no…"

Her legs crumble under and she falls down hard.

Pain.

Phillipe still looks at the lighting card.

Meaghan looks up at the lighting booth, her eyes full of tears.

Help.

She struggles to push up with her arms but quickly collapses.

My leg won't move.

She stares up at the lighting booth again. Phillipe points to a pattern on the lighting card. "Number seven, let's try seven."

He lowers the card from his face. Twinkle lights bounce around Meaghan sprawled out on the stage flooring.

"Oh my God!" Phillipe gasps.

"Help," Meaghan weakly says.

Can't stand up. This so isn't good.

CHAPTER 18: THE SHOW MUST GO ON

Lori stands in a large dressing room where all the girls get ready. She is with Priscilla and a couple other girls in the corps. Miss Nancy enters and looks around. She spots Lori.

"Lori." She says.

She has a folded piece of paper in her hand. She hands it to Lori.

"Read it right away."

Lori's face drops.

Oh no.

She holds the note in her hand and looks at it.

Telegram from my parents again…what is keeping them from seeing me perform this time? Miami or the National?

Her eyes well with tears. She slowly unfolds the paper, certain it's full of doom.

Lori, dress for the solo part immediately. You're on. Phillipe.

She looks over the note again.

I…it's me….it does say Lori.

Her frown turns into pure elation.

I get to dance the solo? I get to dance the solo!

She jumps up and down. The tears in her eyes fall down her cheeks.

Priscilla sees the tears.

"Are you alright? Lori, what's going on?"

Lori can't even speak. She just jumps and squeals. She shows her the note. Priscilla's eyes widen. She hugs her immediately.

Then Priscilla steps back. "I wonder what happened to Meaghan."

Lori stops jumping. Her smile lessens.

Ah, poor Meaghan.

* * * * * * * * * * * * * * * * * *

Tatiana walks down the hallway with several bouquets of flowers. Juliet sees her.

"Oh, you made it!" She rushes over and gives her a hug.

"Of course. Wouldn't have missed it for the world. My daughter is performing. Do you know where she is?" Tatiana asks.

"I think she's in the rehearsal studio. They turned it into a little dressing room for the principals." Juliet points down the hall.

"Thanks. See you after the show."

Tatiana starts to walk down the hall. Paige lingers near the bathroom, pacing. She starts to go in and then stop and turns around. She repeats this a couple times as Tatiana approaches. Tatiana watches her closely. She stops.

"Paige?"

Paige looks at her strangely. "Yes."

"I thought so." She wrinkles her face. "I'm Gisela, I mean… Zel's mom."

"Oh my gosh, hi." Paige extends her hand. "It's very nice to meet you. Zel talked about you a lot."

"Hopefully all good things."

"Of course," Paige says quickly.

"Listen, I know it's none of my business but I know about you."

Paige scrunches her forehead.

"The throwing up?"

Paige scowls, mad. "I don't know what you are talking about. Zel is jealous…"

"I've been there." Tatiana interrupts. "Just like you. Younger in fact."

Paige's face softens.

"I know how hard it is. All the pressure. All the ideas and misconceptions. It's so hard. And you're so young. You think you need to be perfect."

"I do."

"But you don't. Trust me. Perfection is boring. But more importantly, what you were just thinking about doing…"

Paige looks at the bathroom.

"Yeah, I know…done that too, back and forth, back and forth. It's not worth it. What you're doing to yourself right now will hurt you for the rest of your life if you don't stop soon."

Paige looks away and tries not to pay attention.

"Gisela doesn't know this but when I was pregnant with her, I almost lost her. She almost died because my body was so weak from what I was doing. I'm lucky she's alive. And after that day, the day I almost lost her, I vowed to never again make myself throw up."

Gisela walks into the hall, but Paige and Tatiana don't see her.

"Because the price I almost had to pay was too large. Nothing in the world is worth more to me than her. And I am so thankful that someone helped me see that. I went to a clinic and got help. Please let me do that for you. Your life is more important than anything."

Paige looks up at her with big sad eyes. She nods.

"Yes." She fights back the tears which start to flow. "Yes, I'd really like that. I don't want to do this anymore." She falls into Tatiana's arms. Tatiana wraps her arms around her and squeezes her tightly. They release.

"Thank you," Paige says.

Tatiana hands her a bouquet of flowers.

"For me?"

Tatiana nods. "For good luck." She turns and sees Gisela standing there. Gisela runs down the hall and hugs her mom. Paige returns to the dressing room.

"Someone's excited," Tatiana says.

"Just glad you're here."

"You knew I would be." She smiles at her daughter, all made up. "I'm really proud of you."

"Mom, I haven't even danced yet," Gisela says.

"Not for that. For being a good friend and telling me about Paige. You're really going to help her."

"Is everything you said true?"

Tatiana nods, "Every word."

Gisela smiles, "I love you."

"Love you more," Tatiana says. "Here," she hands her all the bouquets, "give these to your friends."

Gisela stares at her mom.

I have a really cool mom.

CHAPTER 19: SHOWCASE

The curtain rises on the stage. The corps dance beautifully and the trio emerges from the side. Kelsi, Paige and Gisela shine. They finish and smile at one another as they exit the stage. Then a pair of white ballet slippers slowly walks out on stage. Each step is strong and deliberate.

In the audience, Mr. and Mrs. Clark look through the program confused. Nadine flips through a program as well.

"But she said she was in the corps. I didn't see her." Mrs. Clark says. "Did you see her?"

"Dear, we've been through this ten times already. No, we didn't see her," Mr. Clark says.

"Maybe we missed her," Nadine says.

"We couldn't have, she couldn't have blended in that much."

Nadine looks up and sees Lori standing in the center of the stage before them. She nudges her mom. Mrs. Clark continues on, "I mean honestly…"

Nadine bumps her again, "What?"

Nadine points to the stage. Mrs. Clark looks up and sees Lori cross her wrists and place one leg behind her.

Lori spots her family in the front row and glows. Mrs. Clark melts. She looks up in awe of her daughter's pure beauty.

In the back of the audience, Meaghan's mom and Miss Jenny stare at the stage and squint.

"That's not her," Meaghan's mom says.

"No, it's not. And this is the solo," Miss Jenny adds.

"But why wouldn't she be there. I talked to her this morning."

Miss Jenny shrugs her shoulders.

On stage, Lori's eyes shine. The music starts and she is brought to life. She dances the piece beautifully. She finishes and there's a huge applause. Her parents and sister stand and clap.

"She's so much better than I ever was at that age," Nadine says.

Lori smiles as she curtsies and looks out at the packed house.

Moments later everyone is on stage and the final bows run through. The red velvet curtains close. All the girls yell and scream.

"We did it!"

"Good job."

"That was amazing."

"I had so much fun!"

Kelsi finds Lori. "You were a vision." She hugs her. "Congratulations, you'll be invited to stay for sure."

Paige and Gisela come over and hug her as well.

"Oh my gosh, I didn't know you could dance like that. Girl, you were holding out on us," Gisela says.

The crowd on stage begins to thin out, as the girls go outside and find their families.

Meaghan hobbles over from the wings on a set of crutches.

The girls all gasp. "Oh my God, Meaghan!" Paige says. "What happened?"

"Good ole knee," she says. She turns to Lori. "You were so beautiful. I'm glad you got to do it."

"Aawww," Kelsi says.

The girls form a group huddle and hug as they make their way back to the green room.

"Roommates for life," Gisela says.

They all put their hands in the center.

"Roommates for life," they all say it at the same time. Then the parents begin to rush backstage to find their dancers.

Tatiana enters the room.

"Hey, how did that audition ever go?" Kelsi asks not noticing Zel's mom right behind her.

"Audition, huh?" Tatiana says.

Gisela turns around and smiles.

"Have some explaining to do, eh missy? Great performance!"

Gisela turns back to Kelsi and scowls.

"Thanks."

Kelsi lifts her eyebrows and smiles. "Gotta find my family. See you later." She laughs and leaves the room.

Gisela takes Tatiana's arm and guides her out of the room.

"Mom, I've got something to tell you," she starts. "You might be seeing me on television soon."

Tatiana raises her eyebrows.

"But first, we need to make a deal.""A deal?"

Gisela nods. "I'll go to ballet school for the season, if I get accepted and if I get to do the tap intensive next summer."

"This is really important to you, isn't it?"

"Yeah, it is."

Tatiana smiles. "Deal."

They hug one another.

"Now, tell me about this TV. thing," Tatiana says. Gisela laughs.

They walk down the hall holding hands.

Lori stands in the dance room and looks around. All her friends are gone. Her parents are off in the crowd and she heads towards them thinking…

Oh England, I miss you. Will I ever be as great as my sisters? Do I even WANT to?

Lori drops her head and walks out of the room. Meaghan looks around at all the girls talking amongst themselves. Just then, her mom and Miss Jenny walk through the door.

"Honey!" Meaghan's mom yells.

She rushes to her and drops to her knees in front of Meaghan.

"What happened? Are you okay? Why didn't you call me?"

"I'm fine. I'll tell you all about it later. I'm just so glad you're here."

Meaghan's mom wraps her arms around her.

"Everyone at the studio is so proud of you. I told them all about how you were chosen as the only soloist," Miss Jenny says.

"But, I didn't even get to dance it."

"Sweetheart, you're a star to me."

"I know, mom. Thanks."

Someday…someday I'll dance that solo. Someday I'll be a star.

CHAPTER 20: CURTAIN CALL

Back in their normal ballet attire, the studio is filled with everyone sitting on the floor as the staff sits on chairs against the mirror and Phillipe stands.

"In a moment we'll be handing everyone an envelope. Inside is a letter which tells whether or not we're extending the invitation to you to study fulltime at NYCB. If you have questions you can ask us, but please know that these decisions are final. And on that note, I'd like to thank each and every one of you for spending the summer with us. I hope you enjoyed your experience and for those of you who will be returning, we look forward to continuing your training. It has been a wonderful summer intensive, one of our best by far. You were all amazing in the showcase and should be very proud of yourselves. If you aren't asked to return for the fall, please don't be discouraged. Keep working! Ballet isn't an easy business and you've all proven that you can handle the pressure. Regardless of whether or not our paths ever cross again, the staff and I wish you the best of luck with your careers."

The girls clap.

"And now, the moment you're all waiting for…the envelopes."

Juliet and the Russian woman stand, each has a stack of envelopes in hand.

Phillipe blows kisses out to the girls.

Juliet and the Russian woman begin to distribute envelopes to the girls who begin to mingle and move around. Lori and Paige are each given their envelopes. They look at one another and nod. They quickly rip open the envelopes and pull out their letters. They each read to themselves:

Paige, we are pleased to invite you back for the fall season to continue your training with the New York Company Ballet school.

Lori reads her letter at the same time:

Your successful summer has landed you a place in the eighth grade. Full details will follow in an acceptance package.

Gisela reads her letter:

Fall classes begin three weeks from the date of this letter. Therefore, acceptance of the invitation must be completed within the week.

Meaghan sits on a chair, her crutches by her side. She looks over her paper:

Enrollment is deferred until a medical release clearing you of your injuries is received by the artistic director, at which time you are invited to resume training.

Kelsi sits beside Gisela and reads her letter:

We regret to inform you that you were not selected for the fall season with the New York Company Ballet.

Kelsi stands up and walks away, biting her lip. She continues to read as she walks. Gisela watches her, then gets Lori and Paige's attention. She nods in Kelsi's direction.

"Didn't get in?" Paige asks.

Gisela shrugs. "Doesn't look like it."

"How about Meg?" Kelsi asks.

"I don't know," Paige says. "Let's go see."

They all walk over to Meaghan.

"And the verdict is…" Gisela asks.

"I'll see you guys when my knee heals."

Gisela smiles. "That's great."

"So, we'll all be reunited then," Meaghan says.

"Not me," Kelsi says. "But maybe I'll come visit." She is still reading over her letter.

"Ugh, it won't be the same without you!" Lori says.

"Well, we have to vow to stay in touch. Email, call, text, Skype. I expect to hear from each one of you at least once a week," Kelsi says.

"Yes, ma'am." Gisela salutes.

Kelsi unfolds the bottom third of her paper. A small note falls out. Kelsi picks up the note and reads it:

Kelsi, I think you have great potential. Spend another year training in ballet technique and return next year for auditions. I'm sure you'll be ready then. Best luck, Phillipe Morin.

She looks up and smiles.
I could. I could be a great ballerina.
She looks at the note again.
I will be a great dancer.
She crumples the note in her hand, and tosses it and the letter in a small trashcan in the corner. She walks back over to the others.

"So?" she asks.

Paige, Gisela and Lori all look at each other. "We all got in," they all say at once. They look at one another and giggle.

"Congrats," Kelsi says. She hugs all three girls.

"And...what was that you just threw away?" Gisela says.

"Oh, it's a no with a note. Phillipe said go train more and come back next year, but I really don't think I'm a ballerina girl. I miss jazz and contemporary. For me, ballet is the technique that really helps me to be better at the kinds of dance I really love. I can't imagine missing my competition season and I kinda want to audition for *"So You Think You Can Dance"* when I'm old enough."

"Return of the glitter queen," Lori jokes.

All the girls giggle.

ABOUT THE AUTHOR

In addition to Tutu Much, Airin Emery has written five other books in the Dance Series, by Lechner Syndications. She is currently working on Visions Of Sugarplums for holiday release. After a professional dance career that included everything from Fosse to Cirque du Soliel she has changed gears and now focuses her artistry on choreography and writing. She maintains co-ownership of a dance studio in the Midwest, adjudicates for competitions & festivals and currently lives in Malibu with her husband, three children, and two precocious dogs.